OUT OF THE BOX

MICHELLE MULDER

ORCA BOOK PUBLIS

Library and Archives Canada Cataloguing in Publication

Mulder, Michelle
Out of the box / Michelle Mulder.

Issued also in electronic format.
ISBN 978-1-55469-328-3

I. Title.
PS8626.U435O98 2011   JC813'.6   C2010-907948-5

First published in the United States, 2011
Library of Congress Control Number: 2010941927

Summary: Ellie's passion for tango music leads to an interest in Argentine history and a desire to separate herself from her parents' problems.

Mixed Sources
Product group from well-managed forests, controlled sources and recycled wood or fiber
www.fsc.org Cert no. SW-COC-000952
© 1996 Forest Stewardship Council
FSC

Orca Book Publishers is dedicated to preserving the environment and has printed this book on paper certified by the Forest Stewardship Council.

Orca Book Publishers gratefully acknowledges the support for its publishing programs provided by the following agencies: the Government of Canada through the Canada Book Fund and the Canada Council for the Arts, and the Province of British Columbia through the BC Arts Council and the Book Publishing Tax Credit.

Cover Design by Teresa Bubela
Cover photo by Getty Images
Typesetting by Jasmine Devonshire
Author photo by David Lowes

ORCA BOOK PUBLISHERS
PO Box 5626, Stn. B
Victoria, BC Canada
V8R 6S4

ORCA BOOK PUBLISHERS
PO Box 468
Custer, WA USA
98240-0468

www.orcabook.com
Printed and bound in Canada.

14 13 12 11 • 4 3 2 1

For my family

ORCA
YOUNG
READER

978-1-55469-176-0 $7.95 pb

Ten-year-old Rosario Ramirez and her family are political refugees from Mexico, trying to make a new life in Canada. After being teased at school, Rosario vows not to speak English again until she can speak with an accent that's one hundred percent Canadian. But when her family's closest friend and fellow farm worker, José, gets sick on the job, Rosario's plan starts to fall apart. Neither of Rosario's parents speaks English well enough to get José the help he needs. Like it or not, Rosario must face her fears about letting her voice be heard.

When she was growing up, Michelle's favorite spot was the library, so it's no surprise she studied literature at university. After graduating, she cycled across Canada, traveled in South America and married the Argentine pen pal she'd been writing to since she was fourteen. She lives in Victoria, British Columbia, with her husband and daughter. For more information visit www.michellemulder.com.

One

"Ellie?"

My parents are staring at me across our dining-room table. Mom's still in her work clothes—a tailored beige blouse and black pants that make her seem confident and professional. Dad has changed from his usual T-shirt into something dressier. They've raised their wineglasses full of bubbly water for a goodbye toast, and they're waiting for me to do the same.

I grip the stem of my glass, trying to figure out how long I've been staring out the window at our bark-mulched yard. I was imagining myself picking raspberries in Aunt Jeanette's garden in Victoria. My parents have finally agreed to let me stay with my aunt for the whole summer this year, instead of just a week. Jeanette says she needs help cleaning her basement—

something she and Alison had promised each other they would do this summer. They had wanted to hold a giant yard sale and give all the proceeds to a soup kitchen where they volunteer. Despite everything that's happened, my aunt's sticking to the plan. I told my parents I wanted to help, because it feels like the last thing I can do for Alison. Maybe they get it, or maybe they're worried Jeanette'll get depressed if she sorts through twenty years of memories of Alison by herself. Either way, I've been counting the days until I get to my aunt's place.

I raise my glass. "To a fantastic summer!" I say.

"To Ellie," says Dad.

"To Jeanette," Mom adds, giving us each a long, meaningful look. She's reminded me often in the past few weeks that I can't expect my aunt to be the same as before, now that Alison's gone. Even though Jeanette sounds fine when we talk on the phone or when she visits, grief might come crashing in on her when summer arrives and she's not busy teaching. Besides, summer is the season of kayaking, hiking and lake swimming—activities she and Alison used to share. I think Mom imagines her curled up in a chair, desperate for company, but personally I can't picture it. My aunt always says that life is nothing if not a great adventure. I've told Mom she shouldn't worry so much, but telling Mom not to worry is like telling her not to breathe. Sure enough, Mom seems sad and tired as we clink glasses, and I scramble to think of something cheerful to say. "I was thinking about what to pack," I lie.

"Don't think too hard," Dad says, his voice cheerful enough to make up for my mother's mood. This goodbye dinner was his idea, and he spent all afternoon chopping sun-dried tomatoes and grating extra-aged cheddar for his gourmet macaroni and cheese, my favorite meal. He doesn't usually try this hard, but we both know tonight is important. "You never know what Jeanette has up her sleeve," he says. "You can't possibly prepare for everything."

"No kidding," I say, digging into my macaroni. One year, Jeanette, Alison and I made elaborate costumes and waved from a float in the Canada Day parade. Another time, we rode horses to a secret waterfall at the top of a mountain. Last year we went camping, white-water rafting and to the opera, all in one weekend. That's what visits with Jeanette have always been like. Intense. Fabulous. And full of stuff I'd never do at home.

Dad and I are smiling.

Mom isn't. Tears are welling up in her eyes.

I feel a pang of guilt, but I grit my teeth. I'm not giving in. Not this time. "Great supper, Dad," I say. Somewhere outside, a lawn mower roars to life, startling us and giving me a few extra seconds to think up a cheery new topic. "You guys'll have a great summer too, right? What did Jeanette call it? The romantic opportunity of a lifetime?"

Mom had laughed when Jeanette said that a few weeks ago, and I'm hoping for the same response now. Tomorrow I want to leave with memories of us laughing together. If I can think about that, I'll worry less about what happens here while I'm gone.

On the outside not much will change, I know. When I return, the lawns on our cul-de-sac will be as green as ever. The air will smell of sprinkler water on pavement, and the neighbors will be walking their dogs.

Our backyard might be weedier. The house was new when my parents bought it thirteen years ago, right before I was born, and they've never gotten around to putting in a garden. Each year they order a load of bark mulch and hire a gardener to spread it out so the weeds don't take over. I pull out the dandelions and grasses that sprout through the mulch. Not many do.

It's hard to say what things will be like inside our house two months from now. Mom gets upset a lot, and Dad says no one can calm her down like I can. Dad spends most of his time downstairs in his office, designing software for his company or just surfing the Internet. Mom says no one gets him out of his shell like I do.

I want my parents to laugh now so I can think about that laughter on the ferry ride to Victoria tomorrow.

But Mom's tears are brimming over. I look pleadingly at Dad, and for once, he jumps in. "Come on, now, Gloria," he says. "It'll be a great summer, right? For all of us." His tone is more forceful than usual, as though he won't take *no* for an answer.

Mom closes her eyes and takes a long, deep breath. A breath like she taught me to take before math tests. When she opens her eyes, she looks as determined as Dad. "It *will* be a great summer," she says with a confident smile that matches her professional clothing. "And we'll look forward to hearing about your adventures, Ellie. I know you'll have a wonderful time."

I relax. Dad does too. We talk about the kite Jeanette and I plan to build together—an improvement on last summer's design—and about the park north of Victoria where we want to picnic. Then Dad cracks a joke about being the suburb's King of Romance this summer, and at last I hear the laughter I've been hoping for.

Later that evening I stuff a book and an extra toothbrush into the crannies of my backpack. I leave my iPod and my cell phone on my desk. Jeanette has banned both of them from her house. She says technology "takes people away from the moment." Life at her house is all about "being present." I rolled my eyes when she made that declaration. I'm going to miss my music.

(Mom thinks I hate music because I don't always want to practice my violin, but listening to great artists and wanting to practice an instrument I never liked anyway are two completely different things.)

I don't mind leaving the cell phone behind. My friend Samantha is in Tasmania visiting relatives for the summer, and the only other person who ever calls me is my mother.

I take a last look around my room and ease the zipper shut on my backpack.

Tomorrow I will step into a completely different life.

Two

Jeanette lives in a red wooden house with stained glass windows, four blocks from the ocean. This is my first time back here since Alison's funeral, and the house seems half empty without her. I can't believe she'll never wander into the living room again to read us a funny line from a book. She'll never whip up another batch of double-fudge brownies or create hilarious names for the new dishes she concocts for supper. I want to hear her laugh at Jeanette's wacky ideas or have her chase me around the house in a tickle attack. At home with my parents, I could pretend that she hadn't really died, but here, her absence is everywhere.

I was right about Jeanette though. Every now and then she looks sad, but since I got here this morning, she hasn't spent a single second curled up in her chair, grief-stricken. She's got too many plans. Like tonight, for example.

"You'll love it," she says, twirling across her living room, her blond curls flying straight out and her multicolored skirt billowing around her. She does a crazy weaving side-step across the hardwood floor and finishes with a little spin next to the piano. "Takes a bit of coordination, but you get used to it. Ready to go?"

I laugh. "I don't have any choice, do I?" It's Thursday evening, and for Jeanette that means Israeli dancing under the trees in Beacon Hill Park.

Of course I know better than to protest. As far as Jeanette's concerned, the biggest sin in life is to avoid trying new things. At home, I avoid them as much as possible. My parents think it's best to stick to what you know, and that's convenient for me, because I hate not knowing how to do things. I never want to make a fool of myself. Jeanette doesn't get it; she says perfection is not the point. I tell her that I'm in no danger of achieving perfection anyway.

"Nope, no choice," Jeanette says now, pulling on strappy sandals that lace halfway up her calf. I try to picture Mom wearing something like that, but she'd say they're too young for her, although she's eleven years younger than Jeanette. It's hard to believe Mom and Jeanette are sisters. Even though they are both small and blond, Jeanette is fit and strong, while Mom just looks thin and tired. They both have curly hair, but Mom wears hers short and straightened, while Jeanette either lets her curls billow behind her or gathers them all up into a messy bun, fastened with chopsticks from Chinatown. They could never share clothes.

My aunt grabs a red bandanna from a shelf and ties it on me like a headband. "There's no dress code, but the more folksy, the better, no?" She hesitates, her hand on the doorknob. "You can borrow a skirt or a scarf too, if you want. And I've got some big clip-on hoop earrings."

"Nah, that's okay." I'm willing to try new things this summer, but I draw the line at wearing a full-on costume to the park.

"Suit yourself." She opens the door, and I step outside and take a breath of cool, salty ocean air.

Jeanette lives on a dead-end street with a tiny park at one end and Beacon Hill Park at the other. Her garden is a riot of blossoms; roses climb up the front of the house and peonies as big as my head crowd the path. I'm so busy looking at the flowers that at first I don't notice the girl sitting on the steps of the house next door.

"Hey, Sarah," Jeanette says to her. "It's folk-dancing night. Want to come?"

I cringe. I should have warned my aunt that no other teenager on the planet would be caught dancing with a bunch of crazy adults in a park, but how was I supposed to know that this girl would be sitting outside tonight?

I was excited when Jeanette told me a girl my age had moved in next door. I'd imagined us becoming friends, but one look at her tells me we'll never find anything to say to each other. Especially now that she thinks I'm some sort of folk-dancing enthusiast.

Sarah's obviously not the folk-dancing type. For one thing, she has what I can tell is an expensive haircut. Wisps of black hair frame her face, and her green tank top hugs her in all the places I cover with baggy T-shirts. What gets me most is the huge sunglasses. She looks like a model.

My silly bandanna feels hot and itchy on my head. I prepare myself for her scowl. I'm ready to glare back, link arms with my aunt and sweep us away from rejection.

But Sarah is grinning. She jumps up and grabs the door handle. "I'm there! Just let me tell my dad. Back in a flash."

I raise my eyebrows.

Jeanette only says, "She hasn't missed a single Thursday since they moved here last month."

"Bye!" Sarah calls over her shoulder as she slams out of the house. I've already got goose bumps from the ocean breeze, and she's pulled on a black sweater flecked with silver. I consider running back to get something warmer, but don't want to draw attention to myself. I'll warm up as I dance anyway.

We hurry along the street, past old houses with lush gardens and a fancy new place whose entire front yard is paved over with beige bricks. The rich scent of the park reaches my nose, and I smile. It smells like warm earth and happy plants.

Beacon Hill Park is my favorite place in the whole world. I love the creek by my school too, but this park goes for blocks and blocks, with flower gardens, fields, a hill that sweeps down toward the ocean, and even a petting zoo. We cross a little bridge over a brook, and a peacock's cry slices the evening air. The first time I heard that sound, years ago, I thought someone was being attacked. I'm used to it now. The peacocks are always jumping the fence in the petting zoo and rambling around the park. You can hear them for miles.

"Sounds like George is on the prowl again," Sarah says as we cross the little stone bridge.

"George?" I ask.

"The peacock. He's the one that makes the most racket. The others try, of course, but there's no comparison."

Before I can ask how model-girl knows all this, Jeanette answers my question. "Sarah volunteers at the petting zoo. She's on a first-name basis with all the animals."

I snort, unable to picture her surrounded by smelly goats or mucking out a pigsty. Sarah catches my smirk before I can wipe it off my face.

"It was my parents' idea," she says. "When we moved here, there was only a month of school left. There wasn't much point going for just a few weeks, so I became a petting-zoo volunteer instead. I like it, actually."

"Cool," I say. I mean it. My parents would never let me miss a *day* of school, never mind a whole month.

"Yeah," Sarah says, "but it's not gonna make September any easier. I hate starting all over again."

"You've done it before?" I ask. I never have. Mom moved around a lot when she was little, and she's always made a big thing of staying in one spot while I grow up.

"Seven times," Sarah says. "My dad's a professor. He's always getting jobs at different universities."

Seven? "How old are you?" I ask.

"Thirteen," she says as we come to a clearing in the trees. A handful of adults has already gathered, and their get-ups make my aunt's outfit look almost conservative.

I'm suddenly thankful that Sarah is here, making me stand out less. "I hate it," she says. "Moving, I mean. I'm glad *you're* here for the summer though. At least I'll have someone my own age to hang out with."

The look in her eyes reminds me of kindergarten, when kids ask each other, *Will you be my friend?* It's funny how, at some point, we know we're not supposed to ask that question directly. And it's funny that this girl, who looks like she would be instantly popular at school, is giving me that hopeful look now. I'm not someone that other kids flock to. I don't really see very many kids outside of school, and I never know what to talk about, yet Sarah's looking at me like she'll be disappointed if I don't want to be her friend. "Jeanette's told me all about you," she says. "Did you bring your violin?"

I flinch. I'm not surprised my aunt has told Sarah about me, but did she *have* to mention the violin? It's one of those instruments that isn't very cool, unless you're some sort of child prodigy, which I'm definitely not. "I left it at home," I say. "I'm taking a few months off from practicing."

"Too bad," Sarah says, brushing her perfect hair from her forehead. "I was hoping we could get a duet going. Did Jeanette tell you I play the piano? Jazz mostly, but I'm sure we could work out some kind of violin-piano duet. My uncle has a fiddle you could borrow."

"Cool," I say. I'm trying hard not to gush too much, in case she changes her mind about me, but I can already feel myself hoping we'll be friends. Sarah looks like she lives in a magazine, but anyone who spends her days feeding donkeys and her spare time playing jazz piano would be fun to hang out with.

I smile, and she grins back.

A blast of saxophone and fiddle music makes me jump. One of the full-skirted, hoop-earringed women is herding the others into a circle. Sarah grabs my hand and pulls me into the ring, and soon we're galloping around, bellowing the words to *Hava Nagila* and laughing with all the others.

Three

"Sarah's fantastic!"

The night after Israeli dancing, Jeanette's sitting in the rocking chair on the back porch, staring off into the garden. I've just come back from Sarah's, and I plunk down in the deck chair next to my aunt. "She plays like a professional, and she's got an entire shelf full of sheet music. None of it's classical. All jazz and blues and honky-tonk. I wish Alison could have met her."

Alison loved music. She listened to stuff from all over the world, and I wouldn't know half as much about music if it hadn't been for her. Last summer she discovered the accordion. She immediately went out and got twenty CDs of accordion music, and when she played them for me, she acted like a kid who had just won first prize at a talent show. She even took Jeanette and me to a tango festival, where dancers and musicians talked about the instruments. I didn't expect to be interested, but I loved it all, and I learned that tango isn't just background music for a certain kind of dance. It's a whole kind of music on its own, and you don't need dancers to enjoy it. I've been listening to tango ever since.

Sarah's the only other person I've met who gets that excited about music. Tonight she told me all about Billie Holiday and Fats Waller, and I told her about two of my tango heroes: Ástor Piazzolla and Carlos Gardel. "She's going to lend me a bunch of CDs," I tell Jeanette. "I can hardly wait!"

Jeanette smiles and nods, but she doesn't say anything. I suddenly wonder if I interrupted something, if she came out here to be alone. "How was your afternoon?" I ask.

"Good," she says. "I did a bit of weeding, made a few phone calls, and then came out here to sit for a bit. I was missing Alison."

I wince, wishing I hadn't barged in and started talking, especially about the music Alison adored. I've been missing Alison too, but how can my grief possibly compare to Jeanette's? I've been thinking about Alison ever since I got here, but until now, I haven't mentioned her unless Jeanette does first. I don't want to make my aunt feel worse than she already does. This time, though, I got so excited about the music that I slipped. I place my hand on Jeanette's. "You must miss her a lot," I say, then kick myself for being so obvious and unhelpful. According to Mom, I'm here to support my aunt this summer. Fat lot of good I'm doing her so far.

She doesn't look at me like I'm an idiot though. In fact, she doesn't look at me at all; she just wraps her hand around mine and gazes out into the garden. There are no tears in her eyes, and her voice doesn't catch in her throat when she speaks. "It's when I do our favorite things—picking raspberries or walking by the ocean or sitting here—that I miss her most, but that's when I feel closest to her too. Funny, isn't it?"

I squeeze her hand, and we sit like that for the longest time.

Alison's death was kind of sudden. Not like car accident sudden, but she died within a few months of her diagnosis. I'd always thought leukemia was a thing that kids got, not adults, but Alison was fifty-five, the same age as Jeanette, and she'd seemed healthier than most adults I know. She and my aunt were always kayaking around the Gulf Islands, or cycling through the Rockies, or climbing some mountain or other. Last summer, I got to go with them on a couple of their trips. Alison had seemed the same as ever. It wasn't until October that she started getting sick. By January, she was gone.

The funeral was huge, and Jeanette cried more than anyone I've ever seen, even more than Mom on one of her bad days. But when we got back to the house afterward, Jeanette dried her tears and started telling her favorite Alison stories. Funny things that had happened while traveling or in the years they'd lived together. Pretty soon she was laughing again.

Mom stayed with her for a week after the funeral, and they've talked on the phone two or three times a week ever since. Mom used to take the calls in our kitchen, but lately she's taken the phone up to her home office. When she told me Jeanette wanted me to stay for the whole summer, and that she and Dad thought it would be a good idea, I was stunned. It seemed to come out of nowhere, but I'm certainly not complaining.

"I'm happy you're here," Jeanette says, breaking our long silence on the porch.

"Me too," I say. "I love spending time with you."

It starts getting chilly, and we go inside. She makes some of that instant hot chocolate with the shriveled little marshmallows in it, and I drink it all, pretending it isn't too sweet. Alison used to make it from scratch, thick and rich with cream and melted chocolate, but of course I'd never mention that to Jeanette. Her cooking—which is terrible—is the only thing she has no sense of humor about.

As we sip, we chat about stuff we could do this summer. She grins like a kid, grabs pen and paper, and makes a list for the fridge: canoeing on Thetis Lake, kayaking along the Gorge, cycling to Matticks Farm for ice cream. Jeanette is a big believer in lists. She has lists all over the house, for everything from groceries to home renovations to books she'd like to read. Alison used to tease her about her lists. She said they took all the spontaneity out of life, but Jeanette says they do just the opposite: they help keep her focused on what's most important to her. Sure enough, by the time we go to bed, she seems as excited about life as ever.

I wake up the next morning to the sound of Jeanette's hushed voice. She's talking on the phone. My room is right off the kitchen, and the phone hangs on the wall by her stove. Sunlight is streaming in through my blinds, but I don't hear the birds that usually sing from the cherry tree outside my window in the morning. I wonder what time it is.

"No, that's not necessary," Jeanette is saying. "No, no. Yes, I understand." Her tone is like a brick wall: firm, unmovable. Whatever she's discussing, she's made up her mind and isn't going to budge.

I decide it must be a telemarketer, and I roll over to look at the alarm clock. It's the old-fashioned kind that you see in cartoons, with two hands on a round face, and two bright yellow bells at the top. It's 9:30, the latest I can ever remember sleeping at Jeanette's house.

Morning is Jeanette's favorite time of the day, and she sees nothing wrong with making plans for sunrise. Yesterday, she woke me up at six—which is after sunrise, but still way too early for summer holidays—and we went on a march to end homelessness. By 9:30, we'd already walked ten kilometers and were ready for a second breakfast.

"Good grief, Gloria. It's only a checkup! A couple of months won't make much difference." My aunt's annoyance—and my mother's name—snaps me out of my thoughts, and I sit up, stunned. Jeanette's not talking to a telemarketer. She's talking to my mother.

"Okay, okay. I'll schedule one. We *do* have dentists in Victoria, sis," Jeanette says, her voice gentler, almost teasing.

I blink. How could Mom's own sister not know the effect of that teasing tone? I picture Mom's eyes filling up with tears, and the corners of her mouth turning down—two red flags warning that you've gone too far and need to apologize. But Jeanette isn't apologizing. "I'll find a great dentist," she says. "It'll all work out fine."

I feel sick, the way I always do when Mom gets upset. The calmness of my aunt's voice doesn't match what I imagine is happening at home. If my father or I had spoken to Mom the way Jeanette just has, she'd be sobbing by now.

Unless she's slipped into her Professional Woman mode, the confident, cheerful version reserved for casual friends, marketing clients and people who are more upset than she is.

That must be it, I think. Mom assumes Jeanette is still grieving and heartbroken. Mom is protecting her. She has no idea that my aunt's as spontaneous and goofy as ever. She doesn't know that being sad is part of Jeanette's life right now, but it isn't running her whole life.

I hear the phone clatter back onto its base in the kitchen, and I jump out of bed, moving around noisily and humming one of the jazz tunes Sarah played for me. I try not to think of what's probably happening at home right now. Mom's Professional Woman persona never lasts long when she's at home, and Dad will be the only one around to talk her through her tears this time. I wonder if they'll regret letting me stay here for the entire summer, but I'm glad they think Jeanette needs me more than they do.

I pull open the bedroom door and step into the sunny yellow kitchen. I smell pancakes burning.

The table is already set. An orange bowl of dusky raspberries sits at the center, next to a Mason jar of yellow roses.

"Good morning," Jeanette says, waving her pancake flipper at me as smoke drifts up from the frying pan. "Sleep well?"

I nod and stretch. "Have you been up long?"

"Oh, a few hours," she says, "puttering around."

I hold my breath. If she mentions my mother's call, should I say that I overheard it? Would that embarrass her, or would she expect it, since the phone is so close to my bedroom?

She doesn't bring it up. Maybe she has no idea that, at this very minute, my father is hugging Mom, reassuring her that Jeanette is going through a hard time, telling her she shouldn't take things so personally.

"Did you see the empty shelf in your bedroom?" Jeanette asks, flipping a blackened pancake onto a stack of slightly more edible-looking ones.

"The shelf in the bookcase?"

She nods. "I cleared it out for library books. I thought we could go this afternoon and get you a card."

"That," I say, "is the best news I've heard all day." I never went to the library when I was here before. My time was all about doing things, rather than reading.

That was always okay for a few days, but I'm glad it won't be like that all summer.

I've loved books for as long as I can remember. Mom used to spend hours reading to me. I imagined myself into each story, and we talked about our favorite characters the way some people talk about their friends and relatives. On Saturdays, as a special treat, she'd make baked custard for me because that's what Winnie the Pooh ate.

These days I read whenever I can, and summertime is the only time of year when my life isn't jammed full of school, French lessons, self-defense classes, violin practice and homework. I can spend entire days with my nose in a book—escaping from Afghanistan, living on the streets of Ethiopia or solving mysteries in Halifax. I leave the rest of the world behind.

"Best news all day, eh?" Jeanette asks. "Well, you *have* only been up for a few minutes."

I flash back to the phone conversation. A person can hear way too much in a few minutes, I think. I focus on smiling instead of letting my mind wander back home.

Four

Jeanette laughs when she joins Sarah and me in the teen section of the library. "We can come back again in a few days, you know," she says.

I've completely taken over the nearest table, stacking my selections in neat piles: books about accordions, novels, and a bunch of CDs, mostly tango.

"Don't forget you have to carry all those home in your backpack," Sarah says, and I freeze. How could I forget about the car thing? I'm so used to taking out twenty books at a time that I totally forgot we walked here. At home, nothing is within walking distance, and there aren't many sidewalks to walk on anyway.

Jeanette lives a ten-minute walk from downtown Victoria, where the library is. She has a car, but she doesn't believe in using it unless she absolutely has to.

She walks everywhere or rides her bike or takes the bus. (She even got me a bicycle. We agreed that my mother—who calls cycling a head injury waiting to happen—doesn't have to know.) Normally I don't mind. I like going slow enough to notice things. Today, the three of us meandered downtown, sniffing big white peonies, waving to a toddler who peered at us from the front window of a house, and stopping to listen to a kid play the violin across from the ivy-covered Empress Hotel. He was playing one of the classical pieces that my teacher asked me to learn last year. Sarah said she liked it. I said I'd take tango any day.

Much as I like walking with Jeanette and Sarah, I also like checking out big stacks of library books. The thought of running out of reading material makes me panicky. My parents are always teasing me about my book addiction, but I'm not going to think about my parents. I don't want to feel guilty. Whenever they're fighting, or Mom's upset, or Dad's disappeared into the basement, I wish I were somewhere else. Now that I *am* somewhere else, though, I feel like I should be there, doing something to help.

A chill rolls down my spine. What if Mom called about more than just the dentist? What if she has bigger news, but she doesn't know how to break it to us? What if they're getting a divorce?

Mom threatens it often enough. Is that why they were fine with me coming here? They needed me out of the way while they made the final arrangements?

"I promise we'll come back soon," Jeanette says. "The library's on the way to pretty much everywhere." She looks concerned, and I realize my face is all scrunched up. I must look like I'm three years old and someone's taken away my teddy bear. I shove my thoughts aside and force myself to laugh. Her face relaxes.

Sarah whistles. "You must really like to read."

"Yup," I say, embarrassed. "My parents call me a book junkie."

"There are worse addictions," Jeanette says, rummaging in her knapsack for pen and paper. I write down the names of the books I'm leaving behind so I can find them again later.

I feel better now that I have a book stash, but I still feel weird about this morning's phone call. I keep waiting for Jeanette to mention it, but she doesn't. Again I wonder if the dentist appointment was the only reason for the call, or if there's something more that I'm missing.

I know better than to prod an adult who doesn't want to talk. For instance, Dad never talks about his childhood, but it must have been pretty bad. We never see his parents, no matter how much I ask. He'll talk about anything else under the sun, even stuff that kids never want to hear about—like the first time he had sex—but not his family.

Mom's parents died before I was born. Jeanette is the only blood relation I know. Mom was only six when Jeanette left home at seventeen. According to Jeanette, their father was an alcoholic bully and their mom couldn't stand up to him, so Jeanette struck out on her own, working as a waitress in a coffee shop and sleeping on a friend's floor until she had enough money to rent an apartment. Mom says all hell broke loose in their house after Jeanette left, and things happened that she'll never recover from. Eventually, their father took off and their mother had a breakdown.

Jeanette rescued Mom when Mom was ten and raised her on her own, only going to teachers' college after Mom was in high school and could fend for herself a bit. Despite having all that responsibility, Jeanette turned out fearless and fun-loving. Mom is scared of everything. Now that I'm thirteen, she worries even more than usual. She's forever telling me she understands that rebellion is a natural part of being a teenager, and she knows I'll do my own share of acting out, but she wants me to make wise decisions. I tell her I'm not going to get pregnant or become a druggie or anything, and she looks at me sadly and says it's hard to predict these things. Other times she looks at me like I might turn into a werewolf right in front of her.

Sometimes I wish I could go directly from twelve to eighteen, just to save her the anxiety.

Jeanette, on the other hand, flies at life, ready to snatch up everything it has on offer. If I turned into a werewolf tomorrow, she'd congratulate me on all the new opportunities I'd have in the film industry.

They're totally different, Jeanette and Mom. When they're together, you can tell they love each other, but that doesn't mean they don't fight. Mom never much liked Alison, for example. Every time we came to visit, Alison wanted to hike Mount Doug, or paddle the Gorge, or at least invite a bunch of friends over for an exotic banquet. Mom only wanted to chill, and she seemed to take it personally that Alison wasn't interested in sitting around chatting all the time. Mom never got that Alison wasn't the chatting type. So Mom and Jeanette have had their fair share of fights, and whenever they're mad at each other, I hear all about it. Mom doesn't believe in hiding things from me, and as soon as she gets off the phone with Jeanette, she tells me every detail of the argument.

Jeanette's not like that though. She's not telling me anything about her phone conversation with Mom.

Five

"It's now or never," Jeanette says, flicking on the switch in the stairwell down to the basement. "You're sure you're ready for this?"

I laugh. "*I'm* ready. Are *you*?" I've got on my oldest pair of shorts. They're too small and have faded to an ugly pink instead of red, but they're perfect for cleaning out a basement.

My aunt shakes her head. "Nope. Definitely not ready. Do you have any idea how long this is going to take?"

I shrug and plod down the wooden steps behind her. For as long as I can remember, I've loved organizing. When I was little, I liked to sort out the recipes Mom clipped from the newspaper and piled in a corner of the kitchen counter. Once I offered Dad my allowance to let me organize his office.

Jeanette's basement has always been a mess, full of everything from books about Mexican microwave cookery to bags of stamps from fifty years ago. Everything that's ever interested Jeanette or Alison—and lots of things that haven't—is down here. You never know what you'll find if you move a box or kick aside a pile of magazines.

"I don't mind helping," I say.

Jeanette glances back at me. "You don't have to, you know. Alison would have understood. She never did agree with child labor."

I laugh. "Aunt Jeanette, you're stalling."

She surveys the dark, low-ceilinged room. I can already picture the place empty and swept clean. I feel like an explorer, about to discover new worlds.

"Oh god," Jeanette says, picking up a tattered pink hula skirt. "Where do we start?"

I smirk. "Looks like you just did."

She tosses the skirt onto the stairs—the only available space—and we begin picking through stuff. Behind two boxes of chipped bright orange dishes, I find a stack of books about octopuses. Beyond that is a red guitar case and a reclining bicycle. A bag of tap-dancing shoes sits on top of some mountaineering gear. To the right is a set of golf clubs.

"Golf clubs?" I ask. "Since when—?"

"The putting green in the park. We wanted to use it, since we're so close, and we found a few putters at a garage sale, but the guy wouldn't let us leave without the entire set of clubs."

I nod and hold up a 1972 orangutan calendar. We both laugh.

An hour later, the place doesn't look much different. I've started two piles—one to keep for the sale and one to throw out—and Jeanette is squatting in front of a bookshelf, engrossed in the history of Borneo. I've discovered a black cube-shaped instrument case, less dusty than most of the stuff down here. I blow the dust off and pull gently at the handle. My heart speeds up. I can think of only one instrument—an accordion—that would fit in a case like this, and one person—Alison—who might own one.

I press the latches, and they flip open easily. A soft red cloth covers something too small to be an accordion. I sigh and feel a wave of guilt as I realize what the contents might really be. I didn't get to see Alison while she was sick, but Mom says the whole house was filled with medical equipment. After the funeral, Mom helped Jeanette clear it up. They probably put it all down here in the basement. What I'm looking at is probably some sort of medical device from when Alison was sick.

Instead of honoring Alison's memory, I'm thinking only of myself. I glance back over my shoulder. My aunt has placed the book on the floor beside her and is pulling another off the shelf. She's smiling.

I consider shutting the case, but instead, I peek under the red cloth and gasp. It's not medical equipment, and it's not an accordion. It's something even better than an accordion.

"You found the *bandoneón*!" Jeanette says, appearing beside me. "I brought it down here when we needed more space upstairs, and I lost track of it. Alison bought it right before she got sick."

My aunt doesn't look anything like depressed, so I stop trying to hide my excitement. I know, because I saw one at a tango festival last year, that a bandoneón is a tango instrument, smaller than a regular accordion. It has buttons on both sides instead of piano keys.

"Alison bought it on a whim and was determined to learn how to play it. You know what she was like." Jeanette's smile is bigger now. "She even found someone to take lessons from."

I ask her if I can take it out of its case. She nods, and I lift the instrument gingerly from its box. I slip my hands into the handles and draw the bellows apart. The bandoneón wheezes. I press a button and push the folds back together again. It wails. I pull. *Wheeze.*

Press another button and push. *Squeak.* Jeanette sticks
out one arm, curves the other as though around a
woman's waist and strides like a tango dancer down
a narrow path through all the junk. She grabs the
hula skirt, ties it on and dances up the stairs and back
down. The instrument keeps squawking and honking
like an asthmatic goose, and soon we're both laughing
so hard that we sound like sick birds too.

"I'm so glad you found it," Jeanette says, sitting
on the cold concrete floor, fanning herself after the
laughter subsides. "It's yours if you want it."

I stare at her. I've never told her how much I want
to play the accordion—or something like one, anyway.
Dad hates the accordion because his parents forced him
to take lessons when he was a kid. Which is why I've
never asked to learn. Since last summer, though,
I've been sneaking CDs from the library, downloading
foot-stomping accordion tunes onto my iPod and
dreaming of playing them myself one day. It's not
something most teenagers dream about, I know, but
I don't really care. My music makes me happy.

I like the sound of the bandoneón even better
than the accordion. It's richer and more haunting
somehow, and you can add all sorts of accents to the
music by clicking your fingernails across the buttons,
drumming on the casing or bouncing the bellows on
your knee.

"I can't believe you're giving it to me."

"Of course you can have it," she says. "What am I going to do with it?"

"Sell it?" I ask. "It must be worth a fortune." Much as I want this instrument, I know the money should go to the soup kitchen. That's what Alison wanted to do with the basement stuff, wasn't it?

Jeanette shrugs. "We didn't pay much for it. We got it at a yard sale from a woman who kept complaining about all the junk her son brought home. Alison was about to tell her that this 'junk' goes for thousands on eBay when the woman said something racist about a customer who was trying to barter. Alison was so disgusted, she just paid the asking price and left."

I laugh, because I can totally picture Alison's polite smile getting tighter and tighter, rage blazing in her eyes. She didn't get angry often, but when she did, everyone knew it.

"So it *could* be worth a fortune," I say.

"A few thousand," Jeanette admits, "but I think Alison would have wanted you to have it. The idea was to do something useful with our old stuff. Fundraising for the soup kitchen is one possibility. Giving it to someone who would really appreciate it is another."

I nod, looking down at the instrument with its shiny black ends and round white buttons. I do appreciate it, and I can always give it back if I decide it should be sold. For now, it's mine. "Thank you."

I pack it away, smoothing the red cloth on top. Then I take it up to my room, lay it in the center of my bed and give it a pat before heading back down to rescue my aunt from a box of old socks.

"The basement?" Mom asks that evening during our nightly phone call. I settle into the worn armchair by the wall phone. My aunt is the only person I know who doesn't have a cordless phone. Mom's voice sounds tinny and very far away. "I can't believe you've started already," she says. "I thought for sure Jeanette would take a few months to work up to it."

Which shows how little my mother understands her sister. When my aunt says she'll do something, she follows through. No way am I going to point that out, though, because if I say this about Jeanette, Mom will think I'm saying she herself doesn't follow through on things. (Which is true, actually, especially when she's stressed out, but I would never say that aloud. My mom has a lot of great qualities, but it's best to avoid talking about things that aren't her strengths.) "It was raining too much to do anything else today," I tell her. "You should see some of the stuff we found down there!"

For a second, I'm tempted to tell her about the bandoneón, but I stop myself. Depending on Mom's mood, she might see it as a quaint passing interest, or serious competition for the violin, which she knows I hate. She knows how much Dad hates the accordion too, and since I'm not in the mood for another lecture about teenage rebellion, I say nothing.

"You sound like you're having fun." She doesn't sound particularly happy about it.

"Oh, I am," I say too quickly, then rush to cover up before her feelings get hurt. "I miss you though. Are you doing okay?"

There's a long silence, and I can hear her swallow.

"What?" I ask. "What is it?"

Jeanette comes to the door of the living room with a kitchen towel in one hand. She scans my face, and I try to smile to show her that everything's all right, but I can tell Mom's on the verge of tears. The silence, and her swallowing, conjures up the image of her face, eyes scrunched together, lips pressed tight. I know she's shaking her head. "It's just so hard without you," she says. "Your father disappears into his office all the time. Our agreement about chores has just fallen by the wayside."

"Oh, Mom, I'm sorry." I thought it would work so well, the list of chores I'd put on the fridge for them.

"I'm in survival mode." Mom sniffs. Her voice is shaky, but she's fought back the tears for the moment. A few years ago, when I started having panic attacks before math tests, she taught me deep breathing techniques, and we started doing yoga and meditation together. She taught me about pulling into a quiet place inside myself where I was safe and strong and able to do anything I put my mind to. I wish she would remember some of those techniques right now.

Jeanette's frowning at me.

"Maybe if you talk to him," I tell Mom. "Calmly, I mean, and—"

"Ellie," Jeanette says, holding out her hand for the phone. "I've just remembered something that I need to tell your mother." The look on her face says I don't have a choice. I mumble something to Mom and hand over the phone.

"On second thought, I'll use the upstairs phone. Hang up down here when I pick up, Ellie," Jeanette says and bounds up to her bedroom. It doesn't make sense. Surely my aunt can talk to my mother in front of me. What is it that she doesn't want me to know?

Six

"Morning, guys," Jeanette says to four men sprawled on the steps of the stone church. They're scruffy, dressed in far more clothing than most people wear in July, their faces hardened into scowls. But when they see Jeanette, a few of them break into smiles. One guy is missing two front teeth.

I've seen people like this before. They're the ones my parents cross the street to get away from in downtown Vancouver. Of course, when Jeanette wanted me to go with her to the soup kitchen where she volunteers, I knew we'd see people like this, but I hadn't imagined actually talking to them.

Sarah might have imagined it, though, considering the outfit she picked out for me for today. She's a strong believer in outfits that fit the situation and she has the closet to prove it. For my trip to the soup kitchen, she gave me scruffy runners, baggy cutoffs held up with a wide black belt, and a white T-shirt with the sleeves rolled up. "Tough and street-smart," she said, waving me out the door. She pulled a backward ballcap down on my head and looked very proud of her creation. Jeanette seemed more amused than anything else, but she didn't say anything, either for or against, on our way here.

I've already decided not to tell my parents about the soup kitchen. Normally I brag to them about all the crazy stuff Jeanette and I do together, and sometimes my mother declares her sister insane and makes her swear never to take me white-water rafting or tree-climbing or tenting in bear territory again. Jeanette never promises anything, and Mom eventually gives up. Jeanette is the only person who can get my mother to admit defeat. We all laugh about it. I hope that never changes.

"Got a new recruit?" one of the men asks in a gravelly voice. He smells of cigarettes and stale sweat.

"This is my niece, Ellie," says my aunt. "She's staying with me for a couple of months. I wanted to show her where I spend my Monday mornings." She looks at me like I'm supposed to do something. I mumble "Hello" and am about to shove my hands in my pockets when she clears her throat.

It's a threatening kind of sound, one I've heard from teachers at school, but not one that's ever directed at me. I hunch deeper into my costume, but "looking the part," as Sarah says, doesn't make things any easier. I don't know what Jeanette expects me to do.

"Ellie Saunders," she whispers. "*Where are your manners?*"

I look at her, wide-eyed, hoping she'll realize how ridiculous she's being. Does she honestly expect me to shake hands with these people? Mom would be horrified. Much as she believes in politeness, safety always comes first, and who knows if these people ever wash their hands or what they last touched. Yuck.

My aunt's stare reaches out, grabs my stomach and twists it hard. I open my mouth, but no words come.

"Hey, don't be so hard on the kid," says one of the guys.

"Yeah, give her a break," says another. "It's not like I'm the king of France or something." He smirks, and the others snicker like he's made a great joke.

I sneak a glance at Jeanette and can tell I'm beaten. The only thing worse than shaking hands with these men would be to lose her respect. I stick out my hand and smile as though I'm greeting royalty after all. "Pleased to meet you," I lie as I shake hand after filthy hand. There's always soap.

Inside, the building is not the dark, dingy place I had imagined. It's new and bright, with high ceilings and lots of windows, and people sit at long plastic tables, talking, drinking coffee and laughing together. A few people have their heads down, sleeping. One guy is talking to himself. In the far corner, a woman is dancing. Someone else is shouting about poison in the coffee. No one pays any attention to her or to the woman barfing into the garbage can in the corner.

Jeanette tells me this is the lounge, and the soup kitchen and dining hall are up the flight of stairs in the center of the room. As we make our way there, heads turn and people watch us. I don't know if I should look friendly or tough—*show no fear*, like they say in self-defense class. Jeanette is walking straight and tall like she always does, smiling and saying hello to people. She knows a lot of them by name. Suddenly I imagine her coming here with Alison, the two of them walking in and stopping to chat along the way. I pull myself taller and follow Jeanette up the stairs.

The kitchen gleams—metal appliances and white walls. The other three volunteers are all Jeanette's age or even older. The one woman, Louise, has tanned skin and bright white hair. One guy has an army-style brush cut and is in a wheelchair, and the third volunteer is a man whose wrinkled face reminds me of a turtle. They tell me their names too, but minutes later I've forgotten.

Louise shows me where to wash my hands, and then we start making sandwiches. As I smear margarine on hundreds of slices, I keep sneaking glances at my aunt. She's smiling like nothing happened out there on the church steps. I can't even see anger simmering in her eyes. She's much better at hiding it than my parents, I guess, or maybe I just don't know her as well. I'm not looking forward to our walk home, although maybe she'll wait until we're behind the closed doors of her house to ream me out.

"Ned's looking good these days, eh?" she says to the others, then catches my eye and tells me Ned's the guy with the earring we met as we came in. I nod as if I noticed that kind of detail, and she goes on. "He got out of detox a few months ago and has never looked back."

Louise smiles. "I hear he's moving in here soon." She jerks her head toward the far end of the dining hall. Behind those doors, my aunt has told me, homeless people can have a room for up to three months, until they find a more permanent place to live. To be accepted, though, they have to be sober and looking for work.

"Pretty impressive, considering what he's been through," adds Turtle Guy.

Again, Jeanette fills in the blanks. "Alcoholic parents. On the streets by the time he was fourteen.

In and out of shelters for ages. Finally got into a program for drug addiction, but the program's funding got cut, and he wound up on the streets again. Last year, he got hit by a car. It happened right here, in front of the soup kitchen, and a bunch of people saw it. The driver got out, looked at Ned, made some comment about one less drunk and took off. Left him for dead."

I stare. "God."

"Yup, and that's just one story," says Louise. "Everyone here's got stories like that. Amazing they keep going, really. It's humbling to work here, that's for sure."

I think about that as I keep plopping margarine onto bread. Jeanette goes on smiling and talking, but I tune her out. No wonder Jeanette and Alison wanted to donate money to this place. I've never thought about the stories behind guys like Ned. And when I realize that, I see how dumb I've been. Like anyone would *choose* to live like they do. I shake my head, trying to shake my thoughts into some kind of order.

On our way out, I smile at a few of the people in the courtyard, and they smile back, like normal people.

For the first few blocks of our walk home, Jeanette acts like I haven't done anything wrong. In fact, she even smiles when she says, "I'm glad you shook hands with those fellows on the church steps."

I breathe a sigh of relief.

"One of the biggest gifts you can give people," she says, "is to treat them with respect. You did that, and I was proud of you." It sounds like the kind of Teachable Moment speech most adults would make, but Jeanette doesn't do Teachable Moments. I know she's totally sincere.

I don't do tears, yet suddenly they've sprung to my eyes. I wonder if I'm turning into my mother, getting emotional about absolutely everything. I blink furiously. "I thought you were mad at me."

"For shaking their hands? Why would I—?"

"For *not* shaking their hands," I say. "I didn't want to at first."

"But you did, in the end. That's what counts." She looks baffled.

Suddenly I am too. When I was just visiting for a week or so, I didn't worry about making Jeanette mad, but now that I'm here for two months, the thought of crossing her makes me jumpy. What's worse is that I don't know the rules. At least at home, I know where the danger zones are. For the first time it occurs to me that maybe there are no danger zones here.

Seven

That evening, Mom misses our nightly phone call. I know I shouldn't worry. She often works late. Then again, maybe she had something scheduled for tonight, and she forgot to mention that she wouldn't be calling. Whatever she's doing, I hope it gets her mind off her troubles. All day, I've been saving up interesting things to tell her, little things that might make her smile— like the fact that Jeanette got me a dentist appointment at the end of this month. After half an hour of hanging around the wall phone, though, I'm pretty sure my very punctual mother won't be calling, and I'm relieved when Sarah comes to the door.

She's wearing yet another of her many awesome outfits, this time a white blouse with tight jeans that show off her butt. Her hair is shiny, and she's applied the faintest hint of lip gloss. I stand there in my basement-cleaning shorts and a ragged T-shirt, still puzzled that she wants to be my friend.

She flops onto the couch and asks what treasures we unearthed today.

"My favorite was *Wardrobe Renovation Made Simple*—all about how to make dresses out of aprons, scarves out of pant legs, and bowties out of old socks," I say. "*A Loving Look at Outhouses: A History in Pictures* was pretty good too."

She laughs, and I don't tell her that these books were presents from my mom, because I don't want her to think my family's weird. I'm sure they must have seemed like the perfect gifts at the time. Mom tries really hard to give people stuff she thinks they might like. When she gets it right, she's ecstatic.

"So?"

I look up, meeting Sarah's gaze. I realize I haven't heard a word she's said. "Sorry. What was that?"

"I asked if you want to go clothes shopping with me sometime. For school."

"Oh." I'm not sure how to answer. I could pretend to be thrilled and go along, or I could invent an excuse. But excuses mean lying, and lying is exhausting. Besides, the truth has to come out sooner or later, even if it means she'll declare me a total disappointment as a friend. "I actually kind of hate clothes shopping,"

I admit. "It's genetic. My mom hates it even more than I do."

"She does?" Sarah asks, clearly unable to imagine anyone like this. "Who do you go with then?"

"My dad," I say. "We've got a pretty good system. We go through the store and grab a bunch of stuff that might look okay on me. I try it all on and choose a few things, and we head to the cashier. Once a year. Quick and painless."

Sarah doesn't stop staring. "You let your father help pick your clothes? Tell me you at least go to a decent store."

"The Gap. Sometimes Old Navy. I only ever get T-shirts and jeans anyway. Shorts in the summer."

A look of pity flashes across her face, and under any other circumstances, I'd be indignant, but if that pity gets me out of a shopping trip, I'll take it.

"Oh well," she says at last. "Nobody's perfect."

Now I stare at her, until she bursts out laughing. "I'm kidding, Ellie. You don't have to come shopping if it's not your thing."

I smile as if I knew it was a joke all along. I wish I didn't blush so easily though. I ask if she wants some milk and cookies. She agrees, and when I come back with a tray, she's looking down at her nails. "Do you still have that book about making dresses from aprons?"

I scan her face, waiting for the punch line, but I realize she's serious. "You want to make bowties out of old socks?"

She shrugs. "I like sewing. It could be interesting."

I laugh and tell her I'll go get the book.

Sarah's nothing like the person I first thought she was, and this summer is going better than I ever could have imagined.

⁓

Every day since finding the bandoneón, I've been trying to play it. I still sound like poultry with breathing problems, but now and then I get a decent run of notes. Alison would be proud, I think.

And if Mom could stop worrying about teenage rebellion, she might be a little proud too. She always wanted music lessons when she was growing up, which is why she enrolled me in classes almost as soon as I could talk. Today I manage an almost-recognizable rendition of "Twinkle, Twinkle, Little Star" on the bandoneón. I let out a whoop and drop onto the bed, grinning. The instrument case falls off the bed and lands on the floor. For the first time, I notice something brown peeping out from behind the red inner lining.

It's a blank envelope, slightly bigger than letter size, full of papers: a map of Uruguay; a bit of paper with a Victoria address written on it; two old-fashioned airline tickets; and more money than I've ever seen at one time. It's not Canadian money. Most of the bills are American, but some say *República Argentina*. The American money alone adds up to almost two thousand dollars, and the numbers on the bills from Argentina are all in the thousands.

I sit back on my bed and stare at the envelope. All my life, I've wanted something exciting to happen to me. People in books are always finding secret notes hidden in library books or messages in bottles washed up on the shore, but I only ever find old receipts or bus transfers. The one time I found a bottle at the beach, it turned out to be wine someone was chilling for supper.

Now, at last, I've uncovered a mystery. Why would anyone leave that much money in a bandoneón case?

I race to explore every cranny of the case and even parts of the instrument itself. I don't know what I'm expecting, but I find nothing more. I tuck the bandoneón away in the closet, slip the envelope into the drawer of my night table and wander into the kitchen, trying to look aimless or slightly bored, in case Jeanette shows up out of nowhere.

I'll tell her about the envelope eventually, of course, especially if I can't find out who the money belongs to. All that money could buy tons of bread and sandwich meat for the soup kitchen, and maybe then I'd feel better about keeping the bandoneón itself. Before I tell anyone anything, though, I want to know more about what I've found.

Through the kitchen window, I see Jeanette in the garden, chatting over the back fence to Mr. Ignilioni, the most long-winded guy in the neighborhood.

I breathe a sigh of relief and dash into the living room. For the first time ever, I use Jeanette's old encyclopedia instead of just teasing her about it. I look up every place name mentioned, and after about half an hour, I've found out that Uruguay is a country in South America, and Argentina is just west of it. Argentina is where tango music started, so I guess it's not surprising that a tango instrument has some connection to Argentina. The airplane tickets are from Montevideo, Uruguay, to Caracas, Venezuela, and the date on the tickets is 22JUN1976. The names on the tickets are Andrés Moreno and Caterina Rizzi.

A knock on the front door startles me so much that I almost fall off the couch.

"Feel like going on a field trip?" Sarah asks when I open up. "I want to check out Vic Middle, the school I'll be going to in September."

I laugh. Can I really be so lucky? A bandoneón, a mystery and a friend who likes school enough to check it out in July?

Sarah gives me a sheepish smile. "I know it's weird, but I want to scope the place out."

"Let me tell Jeanette we're going to school in July," I say with a grin. "Just a sec."

Sarah grins back, and a few minutes later we're heading across the park and up the hill to Vic Middle.

"How's the basement-clearing going?" she asks, kicking a pebble along the sidewalk. "Found any more treasures?"

Her words are like ice down my spine, but I know it's only a coincidence that she's asking, so I play it cool. "I'm still figuring out how to play the first treasure I found," I say. "I'm hoping Jeanette finds plenty of treasure though, preferably expensive stuff that she can sell for the soup kitchen."

We walk along in silence for a few minutes. The farther we get from home, the bigger the houses become. Now we're in a neighborhood of streets lined with enormous oak trees and old mansions, and I'm enjoying the shade. I ask Sarah what she thinks of the sock-to-bowtie book, and she says it's given her a lot of ideas. She looks serious, so I try not to laugh.

For one thing, I'm not sure why she thinks she needs a more interesting wardrobe. Yesterday she showed me photos of herself at various schools. In one shot, she's on an old wooden dock, striking a diver's pose in a sleek one-piece swimsuit. In the next, she's got her hair twisted back and is wearing thick glasses and a long-sleeved dress that makes her look like part of some religious group. In a third, her hair is short and spiky, her clothing black and her face covered in white makeup. In all of them, she's surrounded by what appear to be friends. I know it's silly, but for a moment I wonder if I should pay more attention to my own clothes.

I don't dwell on the thought for more than half a second, though, because we've reached the school. From across the street, it looks like it's all chain-link fence and parking lot, with a patch of yellowing grass at the far end. I squint against the sun.

"Hey, I was wrong about no one being here in the middle of July. I guess you're not the only keener in Victoria, Sarah." Across the parking lot, in the shadow of the school, two boys—one our age and one much younger—are sitting on a curb, poking at the dirt. The older boy holds a jar, and the younger one is dropping bits of earth into it with a stick. They're talking and laughing, and it looks like they're having fun. I'd love to know what they're doing.

Sarah jerks her head in their direction, and we wander closer to the school. Both kids are dark, with thick black hair. The older one is wearing a red ball-cap backward, low-slung jeans and very white running shoes. He looks like he'd be part of the school's cool crowd, not someone who would sit in the dirt with a little boy, talking and laughing. If I were a different person, I would leave Sarah to her investigation of the school and go talk to them.

Sarah is peering in the school windows.

"What do you think?" I ask.

She shrugs. "This art room looks better than most. Come look at the mural."

She stands back, and I press my face up against the glass. On one wall of the classroom, someone has painted life-size images of kids painting a wall of a classroom. I wonder if the kids did it themselves, and what kind of teacher might let them do that. All at once, I wish I were the one coming to this new school. I'd reinvent myself, be braver than I am at home. I picture myself wandering back to Jeanette's place by myself or with friends, spreading out my homework on her sunny kitchen table and listening to music while she chats with friends in the living room or works in her garden. Sunshine and music instead of silence or shouting.

And suddenly I feel like the most ungrateful kid on the planet. Here I am imagining all this when I have a perfectly good home with two parents who need me. I shake my head and try to think of something else.

"Let's go." Sarah steps back from the window. "I've seen everything I need to see."

EIGHT

"Care to come with me?" Jeanette asks. We've just hauled two big bags of postage stamps up from the basement, and she's putting on her sandals and bike helmet. "Louise lives close to Chinatown. Maybe we could stop for red-bean cakes afterward."

"Deal." I slip on my shoes and hoist one of the bags. "Who knew postage stamps could be so heavy?"

"I don't know where Louise plans to keep them," Jeanette says. "Their condo is tiny, and both she and her husband collect all kinds of stuff. You'll see. They're quite the characters."

Louise, from the soup kitchen, and her husband Frank live in a new condo near Chinatown. Louise beckons us in with a big smile and introduces us to Frank, who looks familiar, though I don't know where I'd have met him before. He's short, round, balding, and looks happy to see us.

Their place is incredible. The floors are polished concrete, and the high ceilings are covered in big pipes painted bright orange, red and yellow. A canoe sits in the middle of their living room. "No other space for it," Louise says when she notices me staring.

The usual living-room furniture is squeezed tight around the canoe, and a potter's wheel stands off to one side, leaving very little room to walk. The far wall is full of books—and I mean *full*: floor to ceiling, with a ladder that's two stories tall to reach the top ones. What strikes me most, though, is an enormous poster of a couple dancing, the man in a tuxedo, and the woman in a bright red dress with heels high enough to make walking impossible for most people. I wonder if Frank and Louise were once mad dancing fiends, or if the poster's here because the colors match the decor.

"Tango," Frank says, coming up beside me.

"I know." I ask if he dances and immediately feel my face flush. I can't imagine him and Louise ever looking as glamorous as the dancers in the poster. Maybe he'll think I'm mocking him.

"Used to dance," Frank says. "The music itself has always been more my thing though."

He smiles, and suddenly I know who he is: the bandoneón player at the tango festival Alison took me to last year. I turn to Jeanette, and she's grinning at me. So are Louise and Frank.

"I suspect you two will have a lot to talk about," my aunt says. "This is the fellow who was going to teach Alison to play the bandoneón."

In three days, Jeanette has given me not only the instrument of my dreams but someone to teach me to play it as well. I stand there in stunned silence for a second or two before Louise claps her hands together.

"First we eat," she says. "I've just made a strawberry pie that we can't possibly finish ourselves."

We sit down around the canoe and eat pie and ice cream while Frank tells me about growing up playing accordion in Germany and later studying music in Paris.

"Do you play Edith Piaf's stuff?" I ask, my dessert forgotten, the ice cream melting in front of me.

"Of course. What decent accordion player doesn't play Piaf?" He gets up, goes to a kitchen cupboard, pulls out an accordion and starts to play.

I lean back into the couch and close my eyes, drifting with the strong, sad tones, hearing Piaf's mournful voice in my head. This is way better than my iPod.

"You keep playing like that," Jeanette says, "and this kid'll never finish her dessert."

My pie is now a soupy mess on the plate, but I don't care. I have a hundred questions bubbling up inside me. I don't know where to start, so I begin with the most important. "Can you teach me to play the bandoneón?"

I ask before I think about having no money of my own to pay him, before I remember that my parents won't want a noisy accordion-like instrument in the house and that I won't have time to practice come September. Right now, none of that seems important.

"I was hoping you'd ask," Frank says. "Jeanette tells me you're now the proud owner of a fine instrument. So we'll make a trade. A few lessons this summer for all those stamps you brought over, which will give me many happy hours. Deal?"

I sneak a glance at Jeanette. She nods. I wonder whether she's already made arrangements to pay him. She does things like that: discovering something I'd like and helping me get it. She doesn't care if it's a practical skill. She does it just to see me smile.

I should protest. I should do the responsible thing and ask for time to earn money and pay him. I consider offering him some of the cash I found in the bandoneón case, but he'd probably wonder where I got American money. I could get a news-paper route, or water someone's plants or babysit.

If there's one thing I've learned from my parents, it's not to be in debt to anyone, not even my Aunt Jeanette. But I don't care about any of that right now. "Can we meet twice a week?" I ask.

Louise laughs. "Frank, I think you've met your match."

Nine

"You busy? Want to come to the library with me?" Sarah's standing on Jeanette's front steps with hay in her hair and goat poop on her knees. She picks what I hope is a wood chip off her T-shirt and flicks it to the side.

I laugh and pick the hay out of her hair. "You might want to get rid of some of the straw first, or the herons will take you for a new nesting site as we walk past the park."

"Ha, ha." She flings her hair around, and bits of barnyard fly out. Behind me, I hear Jeanette raise her voice. She's on the phone, sounding unimpressed with the conversation. I assume she's talking to Mom again. Mom's called the past two nights, and we've talked briefly before Jeanette remembers something urgent that she has to talk to my mother about. No one's ever explained that missed phone call. Yesterday I asked Jeanette what was going on, but she told me I worry too much. She had a nervous look on her face when she said it though, and I can't help feeling she's still hiding something from me.

I'm glad Sarah's invited me to the library. I need to get out and think about something other than my family.

"I'll grab my backpack," I tell her. "Back in a second."

"Your aunt let you out on your own today, eh?"

One of the men from the soup kitchen—Ned, the one the volunteers keep talking about—is sitting on the sidewalk on the way to the library. His ballcap lies upside down in front of him, and a few coins glimmer at the bottom.

Sarah raises her eyebrows at me, and I'm not sure what to say. "We're going to the library," I mumble.

"Keep reading, kid," he says. "It'll take you far."

I smile and look him in the eye. He smiles back.

Later, Sarah wants to know who that was. "He stinks."

"You would too if you'd been through what he has." I tell her about the soup kitchen and what I know of his story.

She nods but says nothing more until we walk through the library doors. "I'm headed to the history section."

"I'll be at the computers," I say. I can tell she's dying to ask what I'm up to, but for some reason she holds back, which is good. I'm not ready to share my secret yet.

"Suit yourself," she says and turns down the corridor.

I don't waste any time. As soon as I'm logged in, I go online and google *Andrés Moreno*. At first I get a bunch of personal pages and Facebook listings, but they're all for people in Spain and Colombia. I add *Argentina* to my search and come up with a bunch of websites in Spanish. The first one says *Listado de desaparecidos* on top, and below is a list of names. Screen after screen of names. Thousands of people. I look at another website. The word *desaparecidos* appears again near the top, and it's another list. I do the same search with the other name, Caterina Rizzi, and again I get lists. Then I look up the word *desaparecidos* in a Spanish-English dictionary and discover that it means "disappeared."

I think I understand. They must have been fugitives, in such a hurry to escape the police that they misplaced the bandoneón case with their money and the plane tickets. But how did the bandoneón end up in Victoria, half a world away?

I look up the address that was in the envelope: 78 Oak Crescent, Victoria, British Columbia. Google Maps tells me it's up near the university, but I can't find out who lives there now, never mind in 1976.

I look around at the other computer users—travelers with huge backpacks propped up against their chairs and older people who peer at screens over their glasses. Beyond them, Sarah makes her way toward me, loaded down with books. I quickly flip to my email and log on. Three messages, all from Mom. Subjects: *Miss you, Love you* and *Frustrated.*

I open the last one first. She sent it last night.

To: ellie@channel.com
From: gloria@channel.com
Subject: Frustrated

Dear Ellie Belly,

Sorry we never get to finish our conversations lately. All three times, I've asked Jeanette to pass me over to you when we're done, but she hasn't, always making up excuses. I'm jealous that she gets to spend all that time with you, and I don't even get a proper conversation these days!

My stomach twists painfully. Mom probably thinks I don't want to talk to her, and I had no idea.

All my life, she's been afraid I'd turn against her some day. I read on.

Things here aren't going very well. Like I was telling you, your father's all but disappeared into his office since you left. He comes up for meals and to watch TV, but other than that, he might as well not be around. I get home and want to talk to him, and he just tunes me out. It's like the television is all that matters these days. I have to say I'm getting pretty fed up. If he doesn't pull his weight around here soon, I don't know what's going to happen. Maybe you could call to talk to him. You've always been good at drawing him out. If anyone can get him to shape up, it's you.

Work has been pretty terrible too. So many clients who expect the earth no matter how many other projects I have. I imagine you're having a wonderful time with Jeanette, being a tourist and going on day trips and whatnot. Thank goodness she finally got you a dentist appointment. Sometimes she gets too caught up in having a good time to remember the basics. I wanted to ask you, too, to please work on your math at least a little bit this summer. You know it will help you in September.

*I love you, and I miss you. Please call when you
get this. I need to hear your voice, and I'd really
appreciate your help with your father.*

XOXO Mom

I let out a long breath.

"Everything okay?" Sarah asks.

I nod. Tears prick my eyes. I shake my head. "Things
aren't so good at home."

"What's up?" She shifts her stack of books to one hip.

"I'm afraid my parents are going to divorce before
I get back," I blurt out, stopping myself from saying
the worst part: if they divorce, it'll be my fault. They're
always telling me how much they need me, yet this
summer all I've been thinking about is myself.

Back at Jeanette's, I call home. No one answers.
I leave a message saying I got Mom's email, I love
them and I hope to talk to them soon.

Ten

.

"Before we begin," Frank says, "tell me what got you interested in the bandoneón when most people don't even know what one is."

We're sitting in his living room. A stack of music books rests on the canoe, Frank has his accordion out, and my bandoneón case is unopened at my feet. Outside on the patio Jeanette and Louise are drinking lemonade, and occasionally their peals of laughter carry through the closed door. I tell him about Alison, her thing for tango and the Basement of Wonders. He listens without saying a word.

When I'm finished talking, he says, "I never imagined sitting in my living room talking to a thirteen-year-old about Ástor Piazzolla."

I shrug. "Just because most kids have never heard of him doesn't mean *nobody* has."

"I'm very glad to hear it," Frank says with a half smile. "Glad to hear the world's wrong about teenagers all being delinquents and technology junkies."

I smirk. "I couldn't be even if I wanted to. Do you know Jeanette has an encyclopedia instead of a computer?"

Frank clucks and shakes his head. "An encyclopedia in the living room and a bandoneón in the basement," he says in a loud voice. "She *does* sound like something from another age."

"I heard that!" Jeanette calls. "Don't you have a lesson to teach, Frank Schwartz?"

"Okay, okay." He winks at me and points to my case. "May I?"

I nod, and he places the case on the couch beside him. He lifts the bandoneón out like a baby, caressing the bellows and touching the buttons tenderly. He opens and closes it, playing a few notes, his face full of the same awe that I feel every time I touch it. I smile at him, and he smiles back. "You're a very lucky person, Ellie."

"I know," I say.

He plays a rendition of Ástor Piazzolla's fiery "Otoño porteño," and he totally throws himself into it.

Every muscle in his face is tense, and his body moves to the music. Everything around us falls away, and I find myself sitting on the edge of my seat with my mouth hanging open. I want to play like that, and I want him to teach me. Above all, I want him to know I'm worth teaching.

The piece comes to an explosive finish. I applaud until my palms hurt. He falls back on the couch, exhausted, and the bandoneón case crashes to the floor, the hidden envelope—and its contents—gliding out.

I didn't even plan to bring the envelope, not until the last minute when I was going out the door and it suddenly felt wrong to leave it behind. It had spent decades hiding there in the bandoneón case after all. Separating them now seemed somehow like messing with history.

I'd never let the bandoneón case out of my sight, so it wasn't like I'd lose it or anything. I don't know why I didn't think about what would happen if Frank saw what was in the envelope.

If Alison were here, she would say this happened for a reason. She was a great believer in Everything Unfolding As It Should, and she always said that the key to happiness is celebrating opportunities instead of wasting time being frustrated or baffled by them.

With everything spread out on the floor, though, celebrating opportunity is the last thing I'm thinking about. Frank stares at the envelope and then at me, like I might be a juvenile delinquent after all. I begin to babble, my voice low so Jeanette won't hear, because it suddenly feels weird to have kept this a secret from her. "I found it the other day. Hidden in the lining. I've been trying to figure out where it came from. Like a mystery, you know?" Even I can hear the pleading note in my voice. I don't want him to go all responsible-citizen on me, calling the police or something. "I haven't even told Jeanette yet."

He picks the papers up off the floor, and his expression changes from confusion to shock. He closes his eyes and seems to be considering his words. "Ellie," Frank says, "there's a story here."

"I know." I'm about to tell him what I found online when he asks how much I know about Argentine history.

I wish I'd done more than skim those pages of the encyclopedia the other day. "It used to be a Spanish colony?"

He nods, waiting.

"It's a republic," I add, remembering the words I read on the money.

"All true," he says. "Do you know what was going on in Argentina in 1976 though?"

I want to tell him yes, but I have to shake my head.

"Military dictatorship," he says. "From 1976 to 1983. The military ran the country by trying to control every aspect of people's lives. They censored news, books and letters going in and out of the country. They also arrested people who didn't agree with them, or who they suspected of not agreeing with them—political activists, artists, intellectuals, Jews, and even musicians, because musicians gathered large crowds that the military regime found threatening. The government seized them, tortured them and eventually killed them. Some say up to thirty thousand people were disappeared."

His words hit me like a tidal wave. *Desaparecidos*.

"I found their names on a list," I whisper, suddenly understanding why the plane tickets went unused. "I looked them up on the Internet, and I found out they'd disappeared, but I couldn't find anything else."

Frank closes his eyes for a moment again. "I'm not surprised," he says. "That's what the military was trying to do—erase people without a trace."

What do I do now? I wonder, and I don't realize I've asked out loud until Frank says, "That's entirely up to you. It's your bandoneón."

I think we both know that's not true anymore.

Eleven

"It obviously went well," Jeanette says on the way home from Frank's. "Your fingers haven't stopped moving since we left."

"He gave me a whole song to practice," I say, fingering the notes in the air. An hour of practicing and listening to Frank play has taken my mind off Andrés and Caterina, and I'm buzzing with everything I've learned. "It's a simplified tango tune, and if I practice every day, I think I can do it. Did you know that when you press one of the buttons, you make a different sound depending on whether you compress the bandoneón or pull it apart?"

"Interesting," she says. "So do you think the goose you've been hiding in your room will sound less asthmatic now?"

"Hey!" I poke her. "Watch it."

She pokes me back, and we almost get into a tickle fight on the sidewalk halfway through Chinatown. We stop when we come to the vegetable store that spills out onto the sidewalk. No room for tickling among the densely stacked crates of bananas and spiky, green durian.

"It's good to see you happy," Jeanette says as we pass the giant luck dragon on the corner. "You've had a lot on your shoulders lately."

I frown. "What do you mean?"

"Just that," she says. "Your mother leans pretty heavily on you."

My happiness bubble bursts, and I arrive with a thud in my regular life again. "She's having a tough time," I say. "Dad's not helping out much, and work is really stressful."

She puts an arm around my shoulder and tries to match her step with mine. We used to walk like this when I was younger. Every now and then, she'd jump or kick, and I would laugh and scramble to imitate her. Today I don't change my pace at all.

"You know," she says, "I wish she wouldn't talk to you so much about her problems."

I stiffen. "But that's what families are for, to support each other."

Jeanette looks at me and presses her lips together. "In many ways, that's true," she says. "Especially when everyone in the family is an adult, but right now your parents should be supporting you, not the other way around."

I slow my steps to fall out of sync. She casts me a questioning look and pulls away.

"They do support me," I say, "and I don't see what's wrong with helping them when they need it. I'm not a child, you know."

"Well," she says, "you're certainly wise beyond your years, but that doesn't mean you should have to deal with adult problems yet."

"Is that why you've been taking the phone away from me when I'm talking to Mom?" Anger prickles under my skin. "I have the right to talk to my own family, you know." *At least I treat them with respect,* I want to add, thinking how Mom must have cried after Jeanette snapped at her about the dentist appointment.

Jeanette looks hurt. "I know you do, Ellie," she says, "I just don't think they're being fair to you."

"So you're trying to save me from them?"

Jeanette looks away. We walk in silence for about a block before she says, "I'm not saving you from them so much as from their situation. Ellie, I believe your mom's struggling with some mental-health issues.

And it sounds like your father doesn't know how to help, and the whole situation affects their judgment as well as their emotions."

I roll my eyes. "I can't believe you think that about Mom. She's stressed out. That's all," I tell her. "I should know. I live with her."

"Don't forget I know her really well too," Jeanette says, her tone gentle. "I raised her, and I know what her life was like—all those years with our mom and dad…What makes you think this can't be a mental-health issue?"

"What makes you think it *is*?" I counter, my tone not so soft. "I can't believe you'd call your own sister crazy!"

"I didn't," Jeanette says. "That's your word, not mine. I'm not insulting her, Ellie. I love her too, you know. I'm only saying she's struggling, and it takes more than stress to make a person cry that much or to fly off the handle over things like burned toast."

I flinch. "How do you know about that?" I ask.

A few weeks before I came here, Mom was running late for work, so I thought I'd make her breakfast. I got distracted, though, and burned the toast. When she came into the kitchen, she was furious. I apologized, and that made her madder still. "Good god!" she shouted. "Why are you apologizing? Did I raise you to be a doormat?"

She slammed out of the house without her breakfast. I was stunned into silence for most of the morning, but that evening she acted like nothing had happened. I guess she'd forgiven me, but I was careful about apologizing after that. Mom's got enough on her plate without worrying about having a doormat for a daughter.

"She called me, crying, that night," Jeanette says now. "She felt awful for how she treated you that day, but that's not an excuse. It shouldn't have happened in the first place."

"Like I said, Mom has a lot on her plate," I say, "and she's right that sometimes I apologize if I think that'll make her feel better. I don't see how any of that means she has 'mental-health issues.' She gets up and goes to work every day. She…I mean, she doesn't just lie around and cry or get mad all the time, not the way you make it sound."

"It's not black and white, Ellie," Jeanette says. "Yes, she gets up and goes to work, and she has good days and bad days, but that doesn't mean she's okay. I'm worried about her, Ellie, and I'm worried about you too."

I sigh. Jeanette is paranoid, and maybe a bit jealous of how close my parents and I are. When Mom was growing up, she and Jeanette were super close, but they must have grown apart when Mom married Dad, and Jeanette and Alison got together. Now Alison's gone, and Jeanette's alone. I take a deep breath and try to be understanding.

"I'm not telling you this so you do anything," Jeanette goes on. "Your job is to be thirteen years old and do what thirteen-year-olds do. I only wanted you to know how things look from an outside perspective. I'm encouraging both of your parents to get some help."

She's not asking my opinion. She's telling me what she thinks of my family. What am I supposed to say to that?

I shrug, and we keep walking.

Twelve

"Ta da!" Sarah runs out of her house as soon as Jeanette and I turn onto our street.

My aunt and I haven't said much to each other the rest of the way home. She's probably giving me time to let what she said sink in. I'm keeping my mouth shut, because anything I say might be held against my parents and me. I'm grateful for Sarah's sudden appearance.

She pounds down the stairs and twirls before us in a skirt I haven't seen before, a rainbow of neckties sewn together, and I know right away where she must have got the idea. My mother would be pleased.

Sarah's feet are bare, her blouse is long and flowing, and her hair is tied back in a bandanna. I tell her she looks great, and I mean it. She could wear a potato sack and still look good.

"Thanks," she says. "Wait until you see the sock bowties!"

I laugh, and she asks if I want to go thrift-store shopping with her right now.

"Yes," I say without thinking. Thrift stores have book sections for me to explore while she's trolling the clothing racks, and I couldn't stand another second with Jeanette anyway.

"Here." Jeanette digs in the pocket of her jeans and pulls out a ragged ten-dollar bill. "Go to the gelato place afterward and try out some wacky flavor."

I can't tell if it's an apology or a pledge of ongoing support, but whatever it is, the end result will be gelato, my very favorite dessert. I pocket the cash, leave my bandoneón in my room and take off with Sarah.

⁂

Downtown is crawling with tourists. On the way back from the thrift store, we dodge between shoppers and buskers on the wide sidewalk.

Ned is sitting with his hat out on the pavement. I stop to rummage around in my backpack and pull out a somewhat squashed peanut-butter-and-jam sandwich. I used to think Jeanette was crazy for always having one with her, but after our morning at the soup kitchen, I started doing it too, and now I see why she does it. The grin on Ned's face is totally worth it. "Say hi to your aunt for me!" he says as I go back to where Sarah stands waiting for me.

"You and your aunt are two peas in a pod," she says when I stoop to pick up one of our bags. We've each got a large yellow bag full of colorful dresses, blouses, leggings and skirts, none of which I even noticed until Sarah pulled them off the racks. I did find some great books though. Nestled deep in one of the bags are three books: an old South American guidebook with a big map of Buenos Aires, a novel I've been meaning to read, and another book that I waffled about and finally grabbed at the last minute, *Mental Health and You*. I'm going to need backup to prove to Jeanette how ridiculous she's being.

The gelato shop is only a door that opens onto the sidewalk with a lineup half a block long snaking out in front of it. Behind the door, two teenagers stand between long rows of ice-cream freezers. I order chocolate-chip mint.

"One broccoli with fly specks!" shouts the pimply teenager behind the counter. He rings up the sale while his coworker scoops the gelato.

"Broccoli with fly specks!" the scooper calls back, and I laugh. Alison would have loved that one. She was never much of a gelato fan, but she loved coming here just to hear the crazy names the staff made up.

Sarah orders caramel apple, and the cashier yells, "One mashed potatoes and mud!"

Customers laugh, and someone wonders aloud if they come up with new names for the flavors every day. I'm about to answer that yes, they do—I always order chocolate-chip mint and have never heard it called the same thing twice—when I spot the older boy we saw at Victoria Middle School. This time he's with a kid our age, sitting on the sidewalk, eating a hot dog. They look up and smile.

Guys don't usually pay attention to me, and if they do, I get all tongue-tied and say dumb things. Sarah doesn't seem to worry about stuff like that though. As soon as we've got our cones in hand, she marches up to them. "Hi. Are you going to Vic Middle in the fall?"

"Yeah," says the guy I recognize. "You too?"

"Yup," Sarah says, sticking out her hand to introduce herself. Even *I* know that normal kids don't shake hands, but for some reason, the guys don't even blink. The one I recognize introduces himself as Michael; the other is Steve.

"Ellie here is visiting from Vancouver," Sarah adds, and I smile, like I'm an interesting kid from the big city, not someone who lives in a boring suburb and hardly ever goes downtown.

Sarah sits on the sidewalk, legs folded up beneath her in Lotus position. I plunk down on her other side.

"So what's Vic Middle like?" she asks.

They shrug. "It's okay."

"Good basketball team," adds Steve, adjusting his ballcap.

Michael leans out from behind Steve and looks straight at me. "You look familiar."

I feel my face go hot. Any minute I'll get tongue-tied, and he'll either think I'm mute or a babbling idiot. "A few days ago," I say carefully, "Sarah and I went up to the school to look around. You were there with a little boy."

"Oh, right. My nephew, Jake."

Sarah is still deep in conversation with Steve. Michael's obviously trying to be friendly, and it would look dumb for me to just sit here silently, licking my gelato. "What were you looking for that day?" I ask. "In the dirt, I mean."

"Bugs," Michael says.

"Bugs?"

"Yup," he says. "For my collection. Not that the schoolyard's the best spot for capture, but my sister would only let me take Jake across the street. She's a bit overprotective."

"Oh." I want to ask him how he got interested in collecting bugs, and how he can do it without everyone thinking he's weird, but I'm afraid he'll think I'm nosy. He looks at me for a second, but when I say nothing, he leans back against the wall to finish his hot dog.

Sarah has no trouble keeping her own conversation going. She asks a million questions about Vic Middle and life in Victoria, and within minutes she's writing down Steve's phone number. I raise my eyebrows at her, and she turns a bit pink. "He wants a tour of the petting zoo at the park," she says. "He's thinking of volunteering there."

"Uh-huh," Michael says. "I'll bet he is." He winks at me.

I smile back, for real this time, and hope he doesn't notice my cheeks burning.

Thirteen

To: ellie@channel.com
From: gloria@channel.com
Subject: I love you

Dear Ellie Belly,

I've started this email five times, and I keep erasing it because it comes out all wrong. Mostly, I want to tell you that I miss you and I love you, even if you're mad at me right now. Whatever I've done to offend you, I wish we could just talk it out. I hear your voice, and I know there's something wrong. I'm disappointed in Jeanette for not encouraging you to tell me what's on your mind, but ultimately, you're old enough to make your own decisions about that kind of thing.

I can understand that teenagers get mad at their parents—that's part of being a teen after all—but I've always taught you to talk things out. Punishing me with your silence is not going to solve anything between us.

Please do what you know is right and tell me what's going on.

> *I love you anyway,*
> *Mom XOXO*

I stare at the library computer's screen. How can she accuse me of giving her the silent treatment when I've talked to her every night, except when she didn't call? She must know it's not my fault that Jeanette ends our conversations almost as soon as they've begun. (My aunt still insists she's trying to give me breathing space, but how does she imagine causing problems between my mom and me is helping?)

The woman next to me glances in my direction, and I realize I'm glaring at the computer, jaw clenched and hands balled into fists, my short nails digging into my palms. I close my eyes, breathe deep and try to relax. Above all, I have to remain calm.

I can't do anything right away anyway. Firing back an email is out of the question. When Mom's this upset, all interactions have to be in real time.

I need to be able to gauge her mood and adjust my every comment accordingly.

I glance at the clock on the computer screen. I'm supposed to meet Jeanette at the check-out counter of the library in twenty minutes. I sigh, open a new Internet window, and try to immerse myself in what I came here to do. At first I'm too mad to concentrate properly, but I force myself to focus. I don't want to think about my family anymore.

Andrés Moreno desaparecido, I type. This time, I find a few sites that are more than lists of dead people. One site in particular is a whole newspaper article from 1998 with the name included in one of the paragraphs. I click *Translate this page*, and after a few minutes of deciphering badly translated English, I figure this is what it says:

After a lifetime of believing he'd been born to a marine officer and his wife, Facundo García now knows he was born on July 7, 1976, in an illegal prison in Banfield in the province of Buenos Aires, where his mother, Caterina Rizzi, was being held. His father, Andrés Moreno, was seized on a crowded city bus on June 17, 1976. Rizzi, who was eight months pregnant at the time, was taken from their house two days later in the middle of the night. The young woman gave birth to her child with the

assistance of doctor Jorge Bergés. The baby was deliv-
ered, still bloody and wrapped in newspaper, to
marine officer Aníbal García and his wife Esmerelda
Perez. The doctor then signed a false birth certifi-
cate claiming that the child was born in his private
clinic in Quilmes and that Perez was the biological
mother.

My heart is pounding, and I feel sick to my
stomach. I scan the rest of the article and find the
word *Canada*, followed by a few quotes:

Today, the young man's biological parents remain
"missing." However, more than two decades after
their disappearance, Facundo García has discovered
other relatives and has been welcomed into a
large extended family with members as far away
as Canada.

"I can't express what it was like to meet my
biological grandparents, aunts and uncles for the
first time," says the young man. "They've been
actively looking for me for years, and when I see my
smile on their faces, or my habitual gestures made
by their hands, I realize I've been hoping to find
them too. I just never knew it would be possible."

As for the couple who raised him, he says, "I
don't hate them. It's the deception that hurts.

I've always been honest with them, and all my life they've been lying to me."

I slump back in my chair and blink at the screen. I can't imagine what it must feel like to be Facundo García. No matter how bad my life gets, it could never compare to his.

And no matter how much I want to honor Alison's memory by donating money to the soup kitchen, I can't use the money in the bandoneón case for that, knowing how much Facundo has lost and that I'm holding back one of the few gifts his parents can give him now.

A tap on my shoulder makes me jump.

"I wondered if I'd find you here," Jeanette tugs on the straps of her loaded backpack. "I finished sooner than expected. How are you doing?"

"Uh, fine," I say, closing the window and logging out before she can see what I've been reading. I grab my own backpack and stand up.

"I can wait a bit, if you like," she says, appraising my empty bag. I haven't even looked for books yet, but I don't feel like it now anyway. How can I think about reading when my own aunt is trying to pull my family apart?

I clasp my hands together to stop them from shaking. "It's okay. I've still got a few books at home to read.

Mostly I wanted to check my email." I meet her eyes. "I got a message from Mom."

"Oh?"

We walk to the main exit in silence. Outside, she asks what the email said.

"She thinks I'm angry at her because we never actually finish a conversation these days." I kick a stone in my path. Hard. "She probably assumes I've asked you to take the phone away every evening."

Jeanette sighs. "Look, Ellie, I've told your mother exactly what I've told you: that I think she needs professional help, and that I think you need some space. I asked her to stop telling you all her problems and suggested she look for a psychologist."

I feel like shoving her against the wall and demanding that she use her brain. "If you're so worried about her, why make everything worse by making her think I'm mad at her?"

"Hold on there," she says, stopping to face me. "I didn't *make* her think anything. After you and I discussed the whole mental-health thing, I told her what we had talked about and requested that she not rely on you for emotional support. From there, she jumped to her own conclusions."

"Of course she did," I say. "She probably thinks *I'm* the one who decided she's crazy and that I don't want anything to do with her." It sounds illogical when it comes out of my mouth, but I know my mother.

"If she thinks that, then it's not because I haven't explained." Jeanette bites her lip and is silent for a second. "You know, you could have refused to give me the phone. I wouldn't have forced you to give it to me."

Fire surges into my cheeks, and I glare at her. How dare she make it sound like I'm the one who wants to abandon my parents?

She meets my eyes. "I'm worried about you, Ellie. I think you need a break, and I'm trying to provide that for you. You seem to have blossomed this summer—making friends with Sarah, learning to play the bandoneón, getting to know Victoria on your own. I don't want you to backtrack when you go home."

"What do *you* know about how things work in my family?"

She stares at me in shocked silence. Until this moment "my family" has always included her. I know my words cut deep, but she's brought it on herself. She's asking me to pick favorites, and she should know that's a dangerous game to play.

Fourteen

"Dad, it's me."

"Hi, honey." Dad hates talking on the phone, so we haven't spoken at all since I left home. But I still expected him to sound happier to hear from me. Maybe I've caught him in the middle of something. Maybe he and Mom are working out the details of their divorce. "How's Victoria?"

I describe my adventures with Sarah and meeting Michael and Steve. I do not mention that Sarah has been talking about Michael and Steve almost nonstop since. She sees them as her "in" at Vic Middle. I tell myself it's ridiculous to feel left out when of course they'll be more useful to her than I ever could be.

"That's great, Ellie," my father says.

"How are *you* doing, Dad?" I ask. "Mom says she's worried about you."

"Oh, I'm okay," he says. "Pretty busy with work."

That's always his first answer. It takes several minutes of talking to get to the deeper issues. "Your mother's never home," he says finally, "and when she does get home, she expects me to drop everything and pay attention to her, no matter what I'm doing. It gets old after a while."

"She says she's concerned about you pulling back into yourself."

"Yeah," he admits, "I can see that, but it's a two-way street, you know? She's got to meet me halfway, and not only on her terms."

"Mm." This is exactly what I suspected. Mom never tries to see anything from anyone else's point of view. It's her way or the highway. "Do you know when she'll be back tonight?"

His choking laughter sounds totally unlike him. "Hard to say. She's mostly been calling you from work these days."

"Oh. Well, tell her I'll be waiting for her call."

⸻

"Ellie, it's so good to hear your voice."

You'd think we hadn't spoken in a year. "You too, Mom. Sorry I worried you." I hold my breath until

I can tell if she wants an apology, or if it'll make her angry.

"I've missed you," she whispers, like she always does when she's about to cry. "I just—"

"It's okay, Mom," I say. "I'm not mad. I never was. It's just that—" Damn. How do I explain without making Jeanette look so bad that Mom comes to drag me back? I'm pissed off at my aunt, but not so much that I want to go home. "Jeanette was telling me you were having a hard time and thought you might need some time to think. Without having to worry about me, I mean. That's why she kept taking the phone," I lie.

"And you went along with that?" she asks. "How do you think I've felt this week, sitting here, wondering what I've done to offend you?"

"Mom," I say, "I didn't mean to worry you. I know you're really busy, and—"

"You think I'm too busy to care about you?" Her voice is shrill. "When have I *ever* not been there for you? And as for too busy to care, well, I could say the same thing about you, young lady."

I hate it when she does that. I take a deep breath and put on my calmest voice. "I'm not blaming you, Mom. I know things are very stressful for you at work and at home and everything. I don't want to make things worse."

"So you hide your feelings from me?" She's shouting now. "You think that solves the problem? How would you feel if I treated you that way?"

Now is not the time to point out that I wish she *would* keep her feelings from me a bit more. All at once, I realize Jeanette was right about one thing at least: I could have hung on to the phone all those times, but I didn't.

"What? You're not even going to answer me now?"

"Yes," I blurt, "I'm still here. I'm trying to figure out how to help."

"You don't always have to fix everything, you know," she says. "Sometimes it would help if you just listened."

I don't tell her that I've been trying to do that. What's the point when it's obviously not enough?

Fifteen

Frank, dressed in an orange Hawaiian shirt and jeans, is sitting on his patio reading a book when I arrive. "Welcome, welcome!" he calls.

I grin and wave. The first time I came here, I never would have imagined feeling so at home in this strange, crowded space, but right now this is the only place I feel relaxed and happy. Frank is always thrilled with my progress, and he talks to me like I'm an equal, the way Jeanette talks to me when she's not trying to save me from my parents.

I have to say, though, that Jeanette didn't stay condescending for long. She's stopped asking for the phone when I'm talking to my mom, and we don't discuss my home life anymore. As for Mom,

I've tried to smooth things out between us, but I think she still wonders if I secretly hate her.

"I think I've almost got the song nailed," I tell Frank. "I mean, I know it's probably not very tough, but when you first showed it to me, I thought I could never do it."

"Of course you can!" he says, getting up from his wooden lawn chair. "Come on. Let's get this show on the road."

We settle around the canoe, and I'm about to open my case when he says, "Hey, before I forget, I went to the address you found in the envelope."

"You did?"

"No news, I'm afraid," he says. "The people there just moved in a few years ago, and the family before that was only there for a few years too. No one in the neighborhood seems to have been there for more than a few years."

"You asked other people in the neighborhood too?"

"Of course," Frank says. "That's what a good sleuth has got to do, right?"

I nod. "I've done a bit of sleuthing too." I tell him what I've learned about Andrés and Caterina's son, Facundo García.

Frank goes very still. "So now what?"

I shrug. "I wanted to look up the son on the Internet, but I ran out of time at the library on Saturday, and I haven't been back since." I don't add that Jeanette seems to be keeping me away from the library—and email—whenever she can. She stops short of forbidding me to go on my own or with Sarah, at least. After our conversation about Mom's message, Jeanette and I were silent for a long time, but it's impossible to stay mad at Jeanette for long. By suppertime, we were teasing each other and laughing again, and before going to bed, she came to my room to apologize for meddling. We've been spending all our time together ever since, hiking, cherry-picking or going to the lake for a swim. This morning I had thoughts of going to the library, but she invented some desperate need to find a set of electric massaging slippers that she knew were in the basement somewhere, and she made lunch so late that I had to rush to my lesson.

What she doesn't know is that I'm not interested in emailing Mom anyway. Our last few conversations have left me completely exhausted, and afterward I go to bed only to stare at the ceiling. At about midnight the night after my fight with Jeanette, I pulled out the book on mental health and started reading. The common warning signs of mental illness looked uncomfortably familiar: sleeplessness, changes in appetite, extreme highs and lows, irritability, negative thoughts, excessive worries and anxieties.

And then I found this:

Researchers believe that, in most cases, genetics and environmental factors, such as stress, play a role in mental illness. The sooner one recognizes the warning signs, the better. It's never too early or too late to seek professional help.

I slammed the book shut, shoved it under my bed, snapped off the light and smacked my head down on my pillow. No matter how hard I squeezed my eyes shut, though, sleep wouldn't come.

And my thoughts wouldn't go away.

Nothing I've done has been enough. Listening to my parents' problems. Thinking up ways to make their lives easier. Getting good grades. Trying to be the perfect daughter. What difference has it made? They're still miserable.

Part of me knows Jeanette's right about Mom's mental health, and I'm starting to feel like an idiot for not seeing it before. All my talk of supporting my family, and I didn't even know my own mother was sick. The next day we had another shift at the soup kitchen, and that freaked me out even more. If Mom can develop mental-health issues without me even noticing or being able to help, how far is she from turning into Diane, who hears God's voice, or George, who is convinced that we spit in his sandwich before handing it to him? How will I know when she's at the breaking point?

"Do you want to search here?" Frank asks. "After the lesson, I mean. I've got a computer."

For a moment I don't know what he's talking about, and then I remember that we'd been talking about Facundo García, the guy who had no idea who his real parents were. I nod, and Frank smiles.

"You're a good person, Ellie," he says. Then he fishes out some sheet music from a pile on the floor, and we begin the lesson.

Later, we search the Internet but find only Facebook pages and personal websites of people who were born much earlier or much later than 1976.

Sixteen

Jeanette's basement still has mounds and mounds of stuff that we haven't sorted through yet. At least the "sell" and "throw away" piles are getting bigger though.

"Looks like we've almost got enough for another load," Jeanette says, surveying a heap of broken stuff by the stairs. She's found an artist who turns old junk into sculptures, and once a week, we've been pedaling things across the city to his place. "I don't suppose one of the broken lawn mowers would fit in our bike trailers, eh?"

I laugh. "No way. I draw the line at lawn mowers."

"Okay, okay." She sighs and pulls over a box of vinyl records. "I guess there are some things I'll have to fire up the car for."

"Yup." I scan the stack of boxes nearest me. One is labeled *Costumes (Sound of Music)* and another *Doilies.* I smirk, shake my head and open a plastic grocery bag full of something soft. "Whose toys?" I ask, pulling out a teddy bear.

"So that's where those are," says Jeanette. "We got those for any kids who came to visit, but then we lost track of them somehow. Put them on the stairs. We'll have a toy box in the corner of the living room for visitors."

I'm about to reply when I hear a knock on the tiny window over by the hockey net.

"Are you guys down there?" Sarah calls.

I pop open the window latch, and she sticks her eye close to peer in. "Do you want to go to the drive-in for ice cream later?" she asks. The drive-in is about three blocks away, and going there is a summer tradition in Victoria. I look at Jeanette, and she nods.

"Michael and Steve are going to meet us there," Sarah adds, and I change my mind. I never know what to say around them, and since Sarah asked them first, she'd probably rather go with them.

"I think I should probably pass," I tell her. "We've got quite a bit to do here still."

Jeanette gives me a quizzical look and opens her mouth to say something, but I cut her off. "Maybe another time?"

"Sure," Sarah says, "of course, and, uh, let me know if you need any help down there. I don't mind pitching in."

I feel suddenly guilty, as though I'm the one that's snubbed *her*, and I ask if she wants to join us now. She's around the house and down the steps in record time.

In the next hour, we discover an entire box full of wine corks, a basket of cat toys (in case Jeanette and Alison ever decided to get a cat), and a rock collection. We tease Jeanette mercilessly and laugh so much that by the time Sarah gets up to go, I wish I was going with her, boys or no boys. I can't go back on my decision now though. That would just seem weird.

"See you tomorrow," she says.

"Yeah," I say. "Thanks for coming."

Seventeen

On my fourth Monday in Victoria, I go to the soup kitchen alone. Jeanette has an appointment with her financial advisor.

Things at the soup kitchen are much the same as the first time I went there. The guys are hanging out on the church steps (except for Ned, whom I haven't seen for a while). People are laughing and talking in the courtyard. Someone inside is shouting about poison in the coffee, and when I head upstairs, several people are asleep at their tables.

The other volunteers smile at me when I arrive, and we spend the next hour making polite conversation. Louise tells me that Frank raves about what a great kid I am, and I grin as I slap bologna on slices of bread.

I take my time getting home, looking at all the shop windows that I usually hurry past when I'm with Jeanette. I hesitate when I pass the library. She won't be home from her appointment right away. I could keep researching.

At a library computer, I log in for a half-hour session and google *children of desaparecidos Argentina*. I'm hoping to find more about Facundo García, but I find other people's stories instead, some even more incredible than his. In one, the child didn't want to meet his biological grandparents because he was raised to think they were evil. In another, the biological grandparents didn't want to meet the child because "she had been raised by the enemy." In a third, the child's adoptive family abused him, and by the time he found out the truth about his birth, he hated his adoptive parents so much that he changed his last name and never spoke to them again. I think about that for a few seconds. Then I try something I hadn't thought of before. Instead of googling *Facundo García*, I try the last name he would have had if he hadn't been stolen from his parents: *Facundo Moreno*.

I press Enter, and wait as the slow library computer chugs its way to the Google listings. I know it's silly to imagine finding this guy. Facundo García and Facundo Moreno sound like unusual names to me, but for all I know, they could be the John Smiths of the Spanish-speaking world.

Sure enough, up pops a whole page of hits, most of them personal web pages and Facebook stuff, but this time, there's something else too, something so incredible that it makes me laugh out loud: a page from the University of Victoria's Department of Hispanic Studies. It seems like an unbelievable coincidence, but I know Alison would say It Was Meant to Be.

I click on the UVic site and hold my breath.

The page takes forever to load, but when it does, all the details fit. Facundo Moreno studied in Buenos Aires and Victoria, and his publications are all in the past few years, which would make sense if he was born in 1976. It takes awhile to become a professor, I guess. And wouldn't it make sense that both he and his parents' bandoneón are in the same city, even if it doesn't make sense that they got separated? Then again, Jeanette said Alison got the instrument at a yard sale from someone who didn't even know what a bandoneón was. Maybe it was stolen.

I go over the web page again. On the right is a list of links—Facundo's favorite books, a few poetry journals and, weirdly, a tea shop whose name sounds familiar. I click on it and slowly, very slowly, the computer reveals the events page of a tea shop in downtown Victoria, one that I've passed lots of times on my walks with Jeanette.

Tea Talk. Discover yerba maté, *the ancient drink of health and friendship still popular in South America today. Join us for the fourth of our Tea Around the World lecture series, as Dr. Facundo Moreno, Professor of Hispanic Studies, takes us through this tea's exciting history. Samples and refreshments will follow.*

The date is this Thursday. Three days from now. I imagine Alison looking over my shoulder at the computer screen and laughing. *Don't question it, Ellie. Just enjoy!*

I stare at the page and swallow hard. I could meet him. Without telling him I have his parents' bandoneón. I could just see what he's like and decide later whether I really need to tell him or not. He'll want it back, of course. But I don't know whether I want to give it back. I scribble down the details of the tea talk, shut the computer down, and walk out of the library in a daze.

"You all right?"

I blink and turn to see Ned, or a rough and exhausted version of Ned, anyway. In the two weeks since I gave him the sandwich in front of the gelato shop, it looks like he hasn't slept at all. I dig in my bag for the granola bar I've taken to carrying instead of the sandwich and hand it to him. "I'm fine," I say. "How are you? Haven't seen you around lately."

"Went up island," he says. "Visited a cousin. I'm back now though."

I want to ask if he's still living above the soup kitchen, but I suspect from the haggard look on his face what the answer will be.

"Welcome back" is all I can think of to say.

He thanks me for the granola bar, tips his ballcap to me and wanders off down the street, leaving me torn between his story and questions of how a bandoneón and its owner's long-lost son both wound up in a small Canadian city, thousands of miles from home.

For lunch, Jeanette buys a bunch of salads and packs them into a picnic basket, along with wine-glasses, a bottle of fizzy water and a blue tablecloth. She suggests I invite Sarah, but I say I think she's probably busy. On the way to the park, I ask my aunt about her appointment with the financial advisor.

"Good," she says. "Nothing unexpected." She asks me about the soup kitchen.

I tell her about a woman who said God had told her I was a saint. "I wish she'd tell that to my mother," I say.

"Nah," says Jeanette, "she'd be disappointed in you for going all religious."

"That's true. Oh, and there was this guy who found half a pack of cigarettes on the street and was sharing them with everyone in the courtyard, all excited." We cross the street into the park and take the path around the pond. "I wonder why some people can have terrible lives and still find things to be happy about, and other people can have everything and still be miserable."

She casts me a sidelong glance, and I wish I hadn't spoken. We keep walking, and in the end all she says is "It's all a question of perspective, I guess."

Maybe so, but for the first time, I wish my parents would make more of an effort to be happy, at least some of the time.

Eighteen

Who knew half of Victoria wanted to know about Argentine tea?

The small shop is packed when we arrive, and people are lined up out the door. I've never been in here before, but I like the floor-to-ceiling shelves, lined with black tins bearing names like Rose Burst and Midnight Mist. Alison would have loved it. I imagine her here right now, looking over my shoulder, chuckling at the names and crossing her fingers that this little bit of serendipity turns out to be all that I hope for—not that I know yet what I'm hoping for.

The long counter on one side of the shop reminds me of the pharmacy in a heritage village museum I went to once on a school field trip. At the back of the store, a table is set up on a small platform, and on the table is a round thing the size of an apple with a metal straw coming out of it, a metal thermos and another black tin labeled *Yerba Maté*. One of the employees is brushing invisible flecks of dust off the table.

Jeanette and I squeeze our way through the crowd toward the back. She was surprised at first when I asked if she'd come with me to a talk about tea, but I told her it was Argentine tea, and since the bandoneón comes from Argentina, I wanted to go.

"You're getting into this tango-culture thing in a big way, eh?" she said and left it at that.

My mom, on the other hand, couldn't figure out why I was interested, because she doesn't know about my interest in tango. Her response to the tea talk was, "Your aunt's rubbing off on you," and I wasn't sure what she meant by that, and I didn't ask. I've been watching my step in my conversations with Mom lately, trying not to match her words to symptoms in the mental-health book. It's becoming harder and harder to avoid though.

As Jeanette and I step into the tea shop, I'm not sure this was such a good idea. If this Facundo Moreno turns out to be who I think he is, meeting him will make it much harder for me to keep the bandoneón, and selling it to donate money to the soup kitchen is probably out of the question. I wish I'd thought of that *before* inviting Jeanette to this talk.

My aunt, of course, instantly agreed to come. She's always interested in learning about stuff that has nothing to do with her life. Judging by the number of people she seems to recognize in this room, many of her friends are the same way.

While she stops to talk to someone, I head for the table to look at the round thing with the straw. I read a bit about *maté* before coming today. I know the round thing is traditionally made out of a gourd (a kind of squash with a hard shell), and the straw is called a *bombilla*.

"Got dragged along, did you?" a man says. I assume he works at the tea shop. His long brown hair is pulled back in a ponytail, and he has a short beard and round glasses.

I look around and decide that, yes, he's definitely talking to me. Adults often do that with the youngest person in the room. "I'm the one who dragged my aunt along, actually." I wave a hand in Jeanette's direction. She's deep in conversation and doesn't notice.

"Really?" He sounds surprised. "Do you have some sort of Argentine connection? Or a tea addiction?"

I laugh. "No, no tea addiction. I'm interested in Argentina though."

"Oh?"

"I like tango music," I say. "I'm learning to play it."

"Wow. Now that's something I don't hear every day, especially from someone so young." He has a slight accent, but I'm not sure where from. Quebec, maybe?

"My father played tango," he continues, smiling. "One of my favorite photographs is of him playing something called a bandoneón—it's like an accordion—with my mother clapping in the background."

Understanding hits me like a wave, and even before he introduces himself, I know who he is. He doesn't look like the stuffy, serious professor I imagined, and he seems happier than I thought possible, considering all he's been through.

"I'm Facundo Moreno," he says, holding out his hand.

I shake his hand and introduce myself, my voice catching in my throat. I know so much about him that he doesn't know I know, and I have no idea what to say that won't sound weird. "I guess tango's pretty popular in Argentina."

"It is now," he says. "Not so popular in my father's day though. The government made it illegal for big groups of people to get together, so no one gathered to dance it. A lot of people forgot how." His eyebrows pull together slightly, like he's reliving a painful memory, and I look away to stop from confessing everything.

I glance at my aunt, hoping she'll rescue me, but she's still talking, waving her hands around and laughing.

Someone behind the long pharmacy counter rings a bell for attention. Facundo smiles at me, says he hopes I enjoy the talk and hands me a card. "If you have any more questions about Argentina," he says.

I feel my face go hot, and I mumble, "Thank you." I wish I hadn't come, or at the very least, I wish Facundo were a terrible person who didn't deserve the family heirloom I know I should be giving him.

Nineteen

"I notice you haven't been spending much time with Sarah this past week," Jeanette says one morning a few days after the tea talk. She's spreading a piece of toast with orange marmalade from one of the ancient dust-covered jars of preserves that she found in the basement yesterday. No way am I going to eat anything that old. "Did something happen between you two?"

I stare into my cereal for a few seconds and finally shake my head. "Not really. I've been busy with the bandoneón. Besides, we don't really have much in common anyway."

"Oh?" Jeanette asks. "You guys got on like a house on fire when you first met."

"Maybe we ran out of things to say." I'd rather feel guilty for a white lie than admit to my aunt that I have no idea what to say to the guys Sarah wants to hang out with. I don't want my aunt to pity me or, worse, try to fix me.

"I can't imagine either of you ever suffering from a lack of conversation topics." She takes a bite of her toast, closes her eyes and smiles. "I remember the summer we made this marmalade. It was so sweltering in here that we got a hot plate and did most of the canning outside."

"You helped with canning?" I ask.

"Hey, don't sound so shocked. I do know how to do a few things in the kitchen."

I do a bad job at stifling a laugh, and she throws a tea towel at me. I catch it and throw it back.

"Anyway," she says, "don't change the subject. We were talking about you and Sarah. What's up?"

"Oh, I don't know," I say. "She's trying to meet lots of new people."

"And you don't want to."

"Not really," I say. "Besides, I think she's figured out I'm not exactly Miss Popularity."

"She's ditched you?"

I shrug. "She's always inviting me to stuff, but she invites these guys we met too."

"And you don't like them?"

"They're fine," I say, exasperated because there's no escaping Jeanette when she wants to know something. "I don't know what to say to them, though, and as soon as they find out I like reading and playing bandoneón, they'll think I'm weird, and since I'll be leaving soon anyway, I'm sure Sarah will pick them over me."

"Whoa, whoa, whoa!" Jeanette grabs the edge of the table with both hands. "You've just written off your entire friendship based on what you're afraid *might* happen?"

I slurp the last spoonful of milk and lean back in my chair. "It's not like it hasn't happened before."

"Not with her," Jeanette says.

I shrug. "I should go practice. Frank's given me a lot of work to do."

"Give Sarah a chance, Ellie." She hesitates for a second. "It might be good to have a friend here, you know."

Something about the way she says it makes me look up. Her eyes are bright, but I see tension in her face too. She snatches up the tea towel and folds it into a tiny, nervous square before meeting my eyes. "I wanted to let you know that you'll always have a home with me, Ellie, whenever you need it."

"Thank you."

"What I'm saying is, you don't have to go back at the end of the summer, if you don't want to."

"*What?*" I can't believe she'd take the game of favorites this far, but equally unbelievable is how I'm flooded with images of walking to school with Sarah, doing homework in the friendly quiet of this kitchen and riding my bike to bandoneón lessons for the rest of the year. How can I get mad at Jeanette when I'm obviously so willing to imagine the new life she's suggesting?

"I mean it," Jeanette says, leaning her elbows on the table. "You don't have to make any decisions right now, but I'd like you to think about it. Don't worry about offending me, no matter what you decide. I promise to back you up, no matter what."

I could quit violin lessons, self-defense class and French lessons and just read, hang out with Sarah and practice bandoneón. I might get to go to some tango concerts. If I hang out with Sarah at school, maybe I'll learn to make friends as quickly as she does.

"Think about it," Jeanette says. "I don't mind talking to your Mom if you want me to."

My images of life in Victoria burst like soap bubbles. "What would you tell her?"

"How much you're blossoming here, how you have access to a world-class bandoneón teacher and how much he thinks of your playing."

I wince. "My parents don't know about the bandoneón. I never told them."

"No problem. I did."

"Oh." Now Mom has undeniable proof that I've been keeping things from her. That'll be enough to send her imagination searching for a million other secrets I must be hiding. If Jeanette asks her to let me stay here for the year, she'll be convinced I've become an Uncontrollable Teenager for sure.

Twenty

I need a good twenty-four hours to figure out what to say to my parents. Not about moving here—I haven't made that decision yet—but about the bandoneón.

Withholding information is a big deal in my family. Like I said, my parents believe in discussing everything with me, from their first sexual experiences ("knowledge that might help you make your own decisions") to what they're presently arguing about ("as a member of the family, you deserve to know"). They've always assumed I would be open with them too, and I have been, until now.

"I was wondering when you'd get around to telling us," Mom says when I bring up the bandoneón. "Why did you keep it a secret?"

I can think of no safe way to answer this, so I choose the least painful version of the truth. "I wanted it to be a surprise. You know, I show up at the end of the summer able to play a whole new instrument?"

Mom says nothing at first. "Why wouldn't you want to share your excitement with us, though, as you experience it?"

"I didn't know you'd find it so exciting," I say. "I know Dad, for one, hates anything that sounds like an accordion."

Another long silence. Dangerously long. I brace myself.

"I wish you'd tell me what's going on," she whispers. "You keep saying everything's fine, but if it were really fine, you'd tell me things. Why don't you tell me things anymore?"

I don't know how to respond to that, and I guess my silence lasts a moment too long, because I hear her take a deep breath, and I know any hope of rational conversation is gone.

"I can't stand this anymore," she cries. "We need to talk. I'll get on a ferry first thing tomorrow morning. I can be there by nine."

"No," I say too quickly, then scramble to save myself. "I mean, I'd be happy to talk to you, but no, we don't *need* to talk. Everything's fine. I love you, Mom."

She's crying quietly enough for me to add that I didn't mean to hurt her, and I'd love to see her, but I also understand that work is very busy and I wouldn't want her to fall behind to come over here when everything's—

"Everything's *not* fine between us!" she wails. "I can hear it in your voice."

I cast a pleading look at Jeanette, who's suddenly standing next to me. She holds out her hand for the phone, but I know I have to say something to calm Mom down before I hand her over. "I'm sorry, Mom. I don't know what to say."

"Just let me come," she says. "I need to see you."

"I—"

Jeanette snatches the phone before I can say any more. "Gloria, what is going on?"

Even from a foot away, I can hear Mom's garbled moan.

"Why are you second-guessing your own daughter?" Jeanette asks. "Has she ever lied to you before?…No, she's not. In fact, it took considerable courage for her to tell you how she feels…Of *course* you're still welcome to come. When have I ever locked my door on you?…Forget the poor-me stuff, Gloria. She doesn't hate you. She simply said you don't need to come here on her account. That's *good* news. Nothing worth wailing about."

Jeanette turns and finds me staring at her. She shoos me away with one hand, but I stay rooted to the floor, wondering why Mom hasn't slammed down the phone yet. I think, too, about my dad hiding away in his basement office. I suspect he won't be coming out to comfort her this time, and part of me wants to clamp a hand over Jeanette's mouth. The other part of me wants to reach through the phone and shove my mother across the room.

I turn and run.

Twenty-One

I'm not much of a runner, and by the time I reach the end of the block, I have to slow down. I storm across Douglas Street to the park and head to the stone bridge over Goodacre Lake. Sarah and I often came here on hot days to watch turtles sunning themselves on the rocks. It's a breezy evening now, though, so the turtles have all hidden away, and Sarah's probably holed up with her family playing a happy game of Scrabble. Her dad probably made a chocolate cake, and all five of them are savoring each mouthful, basking in their perfect family-ness.

"Hi there." It's Sarah, of course, the last person on the planet that I want to see—well, second-last, after my mother. She is sitting at the water's edge, poking a stick into the dirt next to her.

"What are you doing here?" I mean it as a curious question, but I admit it comes out a bit harsh.

She looks startled. "Why shouldn't I be here?"

"I mean, I thought you'd be with your family."

"Nah," she says. "Jennifer's at music camp, and my parents and Wylie are watching some movie about dinosaurs."

"Oh."

I sit down on the grass, kind of beside her but a little bit apart. It would be rude to leave, but I don't want her to feel like she has to talk to me either.

Neither of us says anything for a while.

"So what's up with you anyway?" she asks, poking at a bit of algae floating on the water.

I swallow. "What do you mean?"

"Why have you been avoiding me lately?"

I wish I hadn't come here tonight. I wish a giant UFO would suck me up and take me away, never to return. I close my eyes, but nothing happens. When I open them, Sarah is still there, waiting. "I—"

"I was good enough for you when you first got here, but now you've found better things to do? Is that it?"

"What?" I ask. "No, that's not it at—"

"Then what?" She's jabbing at the algae now.

How do I explain that she's got it backward? How do I say that I don't know what to talk to Michael and Steve about, that if it weren't for her hanging out at the petting zoo in addition to looking glamorous, I never would have even tried talking to her? How do I say any of that without sounding pathetic?

"If I did something to make you mad, why don't you just say so?"

"Why is everyone so convinced I'm mad at them, for god's sake!" I'm surprised to find myself shouting.

Sarah jumps up. "Don't yell at me, Ellie. I'm not deaf, and I didn't come to the park to get yelled at."

"I'm sorry," I say. "It's been a rough day." I tell her about my conversation with Mom.

She sits back down. "Sounds like she needs some serious help."

"That's what Jeanette says."

She finds a stone and tosses it into the pond. "What do you think?"

"Maybe. Jeanette wants Mom to see a therapist."

"Think she will?"

"No." I don't tell her that it hurts to think of Mom on a psychologist's couch. Mom always says that psychologists are for people who don't have family and friends to talk to. If I'd listened properly, instead of getting so caught up in my own world, maybe it wouldn't have come to this.

"So is that why you've been avoiding me?" she asks. "Because you were upset about your parents?"

I shake my head and admit that I didn't want to hang out with Michael and Steve. "They'd just think I'm weird. Guys always do, and then you'd have to choose, and I didn't want to be dropped."

"That's the most ridiculous excuse I've ever heard, Ellie. You don't just ditch someone for something they *might* do."

"I didn't ditch you," I say.

"Hard to tell."

"Look, I'm sorry, okay? I can't be perfect all the time." The words—ones that Mom always uses and that I hate—make me squirm.

Sarah tosses her stick into the lake and gets up. "If you ever feel like hanging out instead of feeling sorry for yourself, let me know." She heads back down the path, leaving an emptiness far bigger than the one I'd had when I came to the stone bridge in the first place.

❧

Jeanette is waiting for me in the living room. "I made some tea. Chamomile. For the nerves." She brings me a steaming mug and hands me a plate of chocolate-chip cookies. "These are for your soul. Did your walk help?"

"Next question," I say.

She hands me the plate. "Eat. Very few things don't improve with chocolate." I obey, and she tells me she's asked my mother to leave the next call up to me.

The cookie turns to dust in my mouth. "Oh great. Thanks, Jeanette."

"No problem," she says, ignoring my sarcasm. "Someone's got to stand up for you, Ellie."

I shake my head. "I don't know how you can talk to her the way you do."

"Why not?" She grabs a cookie. "It's a valuable skill to learn, being respectful but firm. And don't forget, she's my little sister—I've had a lot of experience talking to her."

I blow on my tea. "Hate to say this, but I'm not sure how respectful it is if everything you say makes her fall apart."

"Ellie," she says, "right now, anything anyone says will upset her, so we might as well say what we think. She needs professional help. You can't hold yourself responsible for fixing her. Or your father either, for that matter."

We go around and around the same issues for another twenty minutes or so before I tell her I'm going to bed.

The chocolate has done nothing for my soul, and the chamomile hasn't helped either. I stare at the ceiling, trying to remember the last time my parents were both happy. What comes up instead is the picture Facundo talked about, of his father playing the bandoneón and his mother clapping behind him. I imagine them, Andrés with his eyes closed and a little smile on his face, and Caterina grinning. I hope Facundo can hold that image in his mind rather than imagining their faces as they were killed.

I'd like to ask Facundo how he manages to smile, how he can know what he knows about his parents and his life and still find moments of happiness. I want to ask him why my mother, who has a home, work she loves and a daughter who gets straight A's, can be miserable.

Christmastime, I suddenly remember. Right after my violin recital, my parents looked at me like I'd won the Nobel Prize, and they didn't stop grinning all evening.

I close my eyes, clinging to that image, but more recent memories blur it within seconds.

TWENTY-TWO

I sail home from my bandoneón lesson on my old bike, humming the piece that Frank played for me. It's by a Finnish composer. Who knew that tango was wildly popular in Finland, of all places?

I bump up onto the sidewalk and ride through the tiny park at the end of Jeanette's cul-de-sac. As I swing off my seat in front of my aunt's house, I spot Sarah next door, reading on the steps. I say hi, and she raises her hand in greeting but doesn't look up.

I have to apologize, especially if I plan on staying here. I still haven't decided one way or another, but the more I play my bandoneón, or sit in Jeanette's garden, or ride my bike, the more I want to stay. I'll definitely have to learn to cook in self-defense, but how hard can it be? Besides, I'd like to do something to earn my keep.

I wheel my bike through the gate at the side of the house and lock it up.

"Ellie?" Jeanette is at the front door. "Is that you?"

"Yup. I'm back."

"That's good," she says, "because your mother's here."

———

She's sitting in the kitchen, reading a magazine. Her face is red and tear-streaked, but worried rather than angry. Worry is okay. I can deal with worry. I smile big and fling my arms around her.

She hugs me back, but her face remains tense. "You're looking well."

I look down at my faded blue shorts and the old black T-shirt. My legs and arms are tanned, but other than that, nothing about me has changed—on the outside anyway.

"I'm doing great," I say, hoping she'll add *now that you're here* on her own.

She closes her magazine and pushes it away. "Please sit down."

I drop into the chair opposite her. Jeanette remains standing, but grips the back of the chair beside me and offers us tea or juice. Mom shakes her head, her face so serious that for a split second I wonder if Dad's been hit by a truck or something. Jeanette doesn't look grief-stricken though. She looks mad.

"I think it would be best for everyone if you come home," Mom says.

I stare at her. "Now? In the middle of the summer?"

"Yes."

"Why?"

Mom looks from me to Jeanette. Her lower lip quivers dangerously, and she closes her eyes. "I don't want Jeanette turning you against me," she whispers.

The words are like ice water down my neck, but it's what's left unsaid—*I don't want her to take you away*—that makes my stomach turn. All my life, Mom has talked about how Jeanette saved her from their alcoholic father and crazy mother. Now she's glaring at my aunt as if she were a kidnapper.

My mother is being totally irrational, and I know I should get up now and go around the table to where she's sitting. I should put my arms around her, whisper that she's mistaken, and hold her close while she cries. She'll break down and tell us about her problems with Dad, the stresses at work, and her worries about me. I'll prop her up, talk to her gently, and eventually convince her that no one could ever turn me against the mother who's done everything for me. She'll nod, eyes shut as she regains control of her breathing, and finally she'll smile and say thank you. She'll stay for a few days and return home alone, leaving me to enjoy the rest of my summer.

I fold my arms across my chest. "Jeanette is not turning me against you," I say. "Just because I want to spend the rest of the summer here, like we planned, doesn't mean I don't love you."

Mom's eyes fly open. She stares at me, scrunches her eyes shut again and takes a few deep breaths. "I. Want. You. Home."

I cast a pleading look at Jeanette.

"Believe me," Jeanette says, "I've spent the past hour talking to her, but she won't budge. I can't keep you here without her consent."

I close my eyes and try to breathe. "When are we going?"

Mom looks at her watch. "We're still on time for the five o'clock ferry."

"You're kidding," I say. "I'm not leaving just like that! I have friends to say goodbye to."

Mom looks startled. She's spent so much time harping on me to socialize more, and now she seems unable to believe I have friends. "Don't forget Ellie's dentist appointment tomorrow," Jeanette puts in. Good old Jeanette. She's knows how to hit where it counts. Mom is obviously flustered, and Jeanette goes for the jugular.

"You know we'll have to pay in full if we cancel now anyway, and it'll take a few weeks to get her another one at home."

Mom glares at her sister. "Fine," she says through clenched teeth. "But this time tomorrow, we're leaving." She gets up and leaves the room, and I watch her go.

I tell myself everything will be okay. My parents love me, feed me, keep a roof over my head and give me all the stuff they never had as kids. At my age, Mom had escaped from her abusive parents, was living with Jeanette and babysitting to help make ends meet. Who knows what my dad was living through? I really have nothing to complain about.

Jeanette reaches out and places a hand on my arm. "I'm sorry, Ellie."

I meet her eyes, willing myself not to cry.

"You're not a bad person for not wanting to deal with this," she says. "You know that, don't you?"

I nod because I don't trust myself to speak.

"I love you, Ellie," Jeanette says, and I hug her like I'm never going to see her again.

<hr />

Supper is tense—the kind of tension I'm used to at home but that never happens at Jeanette's house.

She and Alison always worked things out before eating together. Mom doesn't care about stuff like that.

Later, Jeanette goes out to weed her garden, and I follow her. As soon as I do, Mom comes out too, saying nothing but sitting within earshot, like a prison warden.

My aunt and I weed silently for a while. I try again to remember my violin recital, when my parents were smiling and life was something to be celebrated. I want to hang on to that image, but I'm not sure I can.

Halfway through the second row of carrots, I make a decision.

"I'm going to make a phone call," I say, wiping the dirt from my knees.

Jeanette nods. Mom looks up from her magazine but does not smile. I walk past her into the house.

Twenty-Three

"All the way downtown, all by yourself?" Mom asks.

"Mom, I'm thirteen," I say. "I have to go out into the world on my own sometime." Telling her I've been doing it all summer—and on a bicycle, no less—will only make matters worse.

"But isn't that box heavy? Are you sure you don't want a ride?"

"I'm fine," I say. "I'll be back in a few hours. Jeanette knows where I'm going."

The box Mom referred to is the bandoneón. I'm taking it to Frank's along with a letter I wrote last night.

Dear Mr. Moreno,

Thank you for coming. I wasn't sure you would, since you only met me once and I wasn't exactly honest about why I went to the tea talk. I know I should have told you about the bandoneón, but I didn't know how. I figured if I went up to you and said I had something that was your father's, you'd probably think I was nuts.

Okay. And there's another reason too. I love this bandoneón and would give just about anything to keep it. But I keep thinking of that picture you told me about, the one of your father playing and your mother clapping behind him. You sounded so grateful for that photograph, and I know the bandoneón would mean a lot to you too. It was something of theirs that made them happy, and it doesn't feel right to keep it from you.

Inside the lining of the case, you'll find an envelope with all sorts of things inside—all the clues I followed to find you. I've left everything exactly how I found it.

I'm leaving Victoria tomorrow. I don't know when I'll be back, but Frank has my email address if you want it.

Yours truly,
Ellie Saunders

P.S. Any idea how both you and your father's bandoneón wound up in Canada separately?

Frank asks me if I'm sure about this, and when I nod, he tells me he's proud and disappointed at the same time. "You have the makings of a damn fine player, and I hate to see you go without a bandoneón. If ever I hear of one for sale, you'll be the first to know, and if you don't go about finding one yourself, I'll personally come over and give you a swift kick in the pants." Coming from Frank, I figure that's the highest compliment. I thank him, he hugs me, and Louise gives me a CD that Frank and his tango group made a few years ago. I promise I'll visit again as soon as I can.

I walk back along Government Street feeling lonelier than I have in my whole life. I eat the granola bar that I brought for Ned and am relieved that Sarah's busy at the petting zoo. Last night I tried to figure out what to say to her, and I wrote a whole speech in my head about how much her friendship has meant to me and how awful I feel about how it's turned out. When I woke up this morning, though, I knew I'd never have the courage to say all that, so it's just as well I won't be able to see her.

In the end, I wrapped up something I found in the basement—a box of my aunt's clothes from the seventies, which Jeanette agrees Sarah will love. The card that I taped to the top said only *Sarah, I'm sorry for being such a lame friend. Hope this makes up for it a bit. E*

I wrote her name on the envelope and left the package at her front door. Sometimes there's only so much you can do.

Twenty-Four

At home, nothing and everything has changed. My list of chores for each person still hangs in the kitchen. The house looks like it hasn't been cleaned since I left, and the only thing in the fridge is half a liter of milk.

The second we're in the door, Dad hugs me, tells me how much he missed me, and suggests we go out for dinner. Mom says he should have had supper on the table by now. Dad stomps off into the kitchen, and half an hour later, we're sitting down to pasta with salmon Alfredo sauce, whipped up with stuff from the pantry and the last of the milk. I smile. No canned soup. No sandwiches. At least in one way, it's good to be home.

My father and I spend the next two days cleaning the house while Mom's at work. I weed the bark mulch in the backyard, walk to the library, fill my backpack with novels and walk home.

I think about the paper Jeanette slipped into my hand before we left: the name and phone number of a counselor, a friend of Alison's who works within a bus ride of my school. "In case you ever want to talk to someone outside the family. Just make an appointment. I'll pay." I don't think I'll call, but I've saved the paper, just in case.

On Saturday, I wake up to the sound of arguing and the growling of my stomach. I ignore my hunger, grab a book from the stack by my bed and try to read. I promised Jeanette I wouldn't get involved in my parents' arguments anymore, and if I show up in the kitchen to make breakfast, they'll want my opinion. It's safer to stay in my room.

When I was at Jeanette's, curled up in a deck chair under the cherry tree on my last night there, I felt like I could stand up to anyone. It was two in the morning, Mom was snoring in the living room, and my aunt and I were having a secret farewell picnic in the backyard. She was talking about setting boundaries and said again that my job is to be a kid. She said my parents need to talk to other adults about their problems, not to me, and that I have every right to tell them that. I wrapped my hands tighter around my mug of hot chocolate and pictured myself standing up to Mom. I pictured her tears, but they didn't hurt me. I felt strong, powerful.

But now, with their shouting ringing in my ears, I'm hiding out in my bedroom, too scared to go out and too hungry to stay. Finally hunger wins out and I go to the kitchen, where Mom is banging dishes in the sink and Dad's leaning against the counter, arms folded, glowering at the floor.

"Don't bother," Mom says when I open the fridge door. "It's not like your father's made the effort to shop properly lately."

"It's been a busy week, Gloria." He sounds more tired than angry.

"So we don't need to eat?" *Clank, clatter, crash.*

I grit my teeth, open the pantry and pull out a box of crackers. I've just found an unopened peanut butter when Mom turns to face me. "Right, Ellie?"

"What?" I bang the jar down on the counter louder than I mean to, and she startles, as if she's the only one around here with noise privileges.

"Division of labor," she snaps. "I mean, this is a family issue, right? So what do you think?"

I think nothing has changed. I think I can try all my life to help them, and they'll keep running in circles, arguing and crying about the same old stuff. My life would be way better with Jeanette, and I wish I'd fought to stay with her. I yank down the page of chores that I'd posted on the fridge and shake it at them. "*This* is what I think. Why bother asking if you're not going to listen anyway?" I crumple it into a ball, hurl it at the floor, grab the box of crackers and slam out the front door.

I walk fast, head down. I don't look up until the rows of identical houses give way to older ones with yards dotted with flowers or vegetables or trees. I pass a llama and what I think is a chicken coop. I feel my jaw relax. I stop white-knuckling my cracker box.

I don't stop walking until I reach an empty lot. It's full of blackberry bushes, and if Jeanette were here, we'd change any plans we had and spend the afternoon picking instead.

The fruit is ripe, the bushes are loaded, and I have an empty cracker box. I'm tempted, but I should be getting back. I've been gone less than an hour, but my parents have no idea where I am, I don't have my cell with me, and Mom is no doubt imagining me snatched up by a serial killer or mowed down by a hit-and-run driver.

I sigh. Sometimes I wonder what she'd do for excitement if she actually lived in reality instead of her head.

I place my box in a bush, propping it up the way Jeanette does, so it won't fall over no matter how full it gets. Then I reach for a blackberry, avoiding the prickles, and pop that first one into my mouth. It's warm and sweet and tastes of summer.

Twenty-Five

Mom's furious at me when I get home. She yells and cries. I hug her but don't apologize. She begs me to tell her where I'm going next time. I agree and head up to my room, pretending not to hear her sniffling. By lunchtime she's pulled herself together, and we all act like nothing's happened.

I abandon my stack of library books and scour the Internet for bandoneóns for sale. I find none I could ever afford, but decide to start earning some money so I'll be prepared when a cheaper one comes up. Besides, staying out of my parents' problems will be easier if I'm out of the house as much as possible.

In the next few days, I find lawns to mow, kids to babysit and a newspaper route. I also make an appointment with that counselor, because it can't hurt, and maybe it'll inspire my parents to see someone themselves. My summer becomes busy. Mom declares I'm wasting my childhood by working too hard (I bite my tongue), but she doesn't try to stop me.

I decide that, someday, I will go live with Jeanette. Not right now, but maybe in a few years, when Mom is better, or at least when she's figured out that I won't try to solve her problems anymore. That's when I'll ask if I can go, and I won't give up until my parents say yes. None of it should surprise my mother: it will be evidence of the rebellious streak that she's been waiting for all along. And I know Jeanette wouldn't mind. She calls every few days now, and she talks to everyone in the house. Other than hers, though, we don't receive many phone calls. No one comes by, either, until the last Friday of summer, when the doorbell rings.

"What are you doing here?" I shriek, flinging my arms around Jeanette, who is standing on our door-step with a bandoneón case in one hand.

"Special delivery," she says. "I figured you might want this before school starts and you get too busy to practice."

"What? How—?"

"May I come in?" she asks. "Or do you expect me to tell you the whole long story on your front walk?"

I step aside, and she marches into the living room. The place looks a lot better than it did a month ago.

Dad and I have been doing the housework together, because Mom's declared that if things ever fall into complete chaos again, she and I will be checking into a hotel, and Dad can expect divorce papers in the mail. The house is now clean, but messy. Mom leaves stacks of paper wherever she goes, and the entire place is starting to look like her office desk.

Jeanette places the bandoneón gently on the footstool and sits down on one end of the couch. I curl up opposite her. "Do my parents know you're here?" I ask.

"Not unless they heard me come in," she says, tucking her feet up beneath her. "Gloria can hardly complain about me dropping by without calling though."

"How did you wind up with the bandoneón?"

"Would you believe Facundo offered to trade it for a broken lawn mower and a china cabinet full of rusted bike chains?"

I laugh. "No way."

"Worth a shot," she says. "Anyway, Frank told him your story, and Facundo wants you to keep playing. He sent a letter explaining it all. It's in the case. He said you'd know where to find it."

I'm fighting back tears. "I don't know what to say."

"*Thank you* will do for starters," she says. "I've got his email address, if you want to write to him. Interesting guy."

"You talked to him?" I ask.

She nods. "Frank invited me along when Facundo came over. You and Frank had quite the sleuthing operation going this summer. Why didn't you ever mention it?"

I feel my face go red. "I was afraid you'd want me to give back the bandoneón."

"But you did anyway."

"I didn't know I would until Mom showed up."

She smiles at me. "I'm proud of you, you know."

"I can't believe he gave it back to me."

"He says it's on loan until you can buy one of your own," she explains. "The only hitch is that he wants to hear you play next time you're in Victoria."

I raise an eyebrow. "Will I be in Victoria again?"

"You will if I have anything to do with it. I'm not going to do all the traveling in this relationship, and you know that house is way too big for just one person."

I rocket off my end of the couch and tackle her in a bear hug.

"Help! Help! I'm being attacked by a teenager!" she shouts. I pull back, laughing, and she tells me Sarah keeps visiting and asking after me. "She's even promised to help with the yard sale. She's going around asking other people on the block if they have stuff to donate too. It's going to be huge!"

Thank you, Sarah.

"She sent you a gift, by the way. It's still in the car, but I'll get it later." She hugs her knees to her chest and smiles at me. "Anyway, Frank and I decided that, if you'll be playing for Facundo, you should probably get a teacher here. Frank's got a pal who lives not too far away who's willing to make house calls."

When Dad comes in, I've got a grin on my face that doesn't at all match the raging tango tune I'm playing. He stands in the doorway listening and doesn't say a word about the horrible accordion-y sound. Instead, he smiles. That evening, while Dad's watching TV, Jeanette's reading in her room and Mom is in her office, I place the bandoneón case and Sarah's gift on my bed.

I take a deep breath and open the case. Peeping out from beneath the liner is a crisp, white envelope. My name is written on the front, and the handwritten letter inside is dated a week ago.

Dear Ellie,

First of all, thank you. My head is still spinning from the twists of fate that brought my father's bandoneón to me. I don't have words to express my gratitude, and so I'm resorting to a rather unorthodox gesture of thanks, which I hope you'll understand.

When I first arrived at Frank's place a few weeks ago, I couldn't wait to touch the same keys that my father, and his father before him, had touched. For years, I've been hearing about this instrument, how my father received it as a gift from his father and played it every night after school for hours. I'm sure he would have become a professional musician if he could have, but as I told you at the tea shop, in his lifetime, the government forbade the gatherings where tango would be played. It seems to me a terrible irony that the government barred him from doing what he loved, yet killed him all the same.

After my parents disappeared, the bandoneón sat in a place of honor in my grandparents' living room, next to my parents' wedding picture. Years later, after my grandparents died, my aunt Ceci brought the bandoneón home with her to Canada. (She had escaped Argentina when the dictatorship first began, and it was she who sent the airline tickets and money to my parents, resources that, unfortunately, they were never able to use.)

A few years before I met Ceci, someone broke into her house here in Victoria and stole all sorts of valuables, including the bandoneón. It was the only memento she had left of her brother, and Ceci was devastated. When she met me and talked to me about my father playing the bandoneón, she cried. She wanted so much to be able to pass the instrument on to me. I never imagined I would someday hold it in my own hands, and I wouldn't have dreamed that someone who received it as a gift, as you did, would be kind enough to give it back.

The envelope inside took my breath away. I didn't know my parents had ever received Ceci's gift. The money would have paid their way in secret across the La Plata River to Uruguay. From there, they would have flown to Caracas, where they could have lived in safety.

For weeks now, I've been thinking about how life would have been if their flight had been just a week earlier. I would have grown up with my parents. They might still be alive today.

I have to remind myself that there's no point thinking this way. Things are as they are, and our job is to make the most of them. I'm donating the money to the Grandmothers of the Plaza de Mayo, who helped me find my biological family. I like the idea that money meant to keep my family together can be used to reunite someone else's.

I also want this bandoneón, which made my father so happy, to inspire another musician. When I first arrived at Frank's a few weeks ago, I felt like I was claiming another piece of my identity.

I wanted only to take the bandoneón and go, but I remembered my manners and made polite conversation with Frank and Jeanette. They told me about you and Alison and how thrilled you were this summer to discover the instrument and learn to play it.

Half an hour later, I thanked them and went on my way. As I was going to sleep that night, though, their words about your excitement echoed in my mind. I thought about you, and about me and my family. Although I have my grandfather's laugh, my father's passion for music and my mother's for books, I am not a bandoneón player. This instrument is my prized possession because if its past, but it was your prized possession because of its future.

And so, weeks after I said polite goodbyes to Frank and Jeanette, carrying my treasure in my arms, I am returning it to you, on loan, until you can find a bandoneón of your own. I know you will take good care of it, and I would love to hear you play, next time you're in Victoria or I'm in Vancouver. When, years from now, you're ready to give it back to me, I will accept it gratefully. Thank you for returning it, and thank you for making it sing again.

Yours truly,
Facundo

I slip the letter back into its hiding place and stroke the bandoneón with one finger. I can't stop smiling.

Sarah's gift is in a box similar to the one I left for her, and a note is taped to the top. *I thought you might like these. At the very least, they'll save you from the boredom of this year's shopping trip. XXOO Sarah.*

Inside is a pile of almost-new clothing, and I soon discover that each piece fits like it was made for me. I don't look like a model, but I do look good.

Maybe this school year will be different after all, I think, admiring myself in the mirror. Then I pick up the bandoneón and begin to play.

Author's note

The military dictatorship in Argentina "disappeared" thousands and thousands of people (estimates range from 9,000 to 30,000). The government and its agents captured people who they felt threatened the dictatorship. Captives were hidden away in secret detention centers, where they were tortured and often killed.

Captive pregnant women were usually kept alive until they gave birth, and the babies were given away in illegal adoptions. Police doctor Jorge Bergés, whose name I use in this novel, attended many of these births and wrote false birth certificates so that the children would never know who their real parents were.

These days, people who suspect that they might be children of the disappeared can find out by contacting an organization called the Grandmothers of the Plaza de Mayo. This group is dedicated to learning what happened to their grandchildren who were captured or born in the secret prisons. Through DNA testing and extensive research, the Grandmothers have identified eighty-eight children who had been given away in illegal adoption. The group will continue its work until they find and identify the other four hundred who are still not accounted for.

Although the military dictatorship in Argentina ended in 1983, years passed before the Argentine government agreed to try the people involved in the kidnapping, torture and killings. Even so, disappearances continue. In 2006, Julio López, who had been held and tortured during the dictatorship, was scheduled to give a final testimony against a former chief of police. Hours before the trial, Julio López disappeared and has never been heard from again.

Acknowledgments

I'd like to thank Dr. Jonathan Goldman, Assistant Professor of Music at the University of Victoria, for his help with details about the *bandoneón*. Thanks, too, to the Canada Council for the Arts and the BC Arts Council for financial support of this project and to Susan Braley, Henry and Alvera Mulder, Maureen Parker, Holly Phillips and Robin Stevenson for support and encouragement throughout writing and revision. I'm grateful to Sarah Harvey for her brilliant editing suggestions and to the whole Orca team for producing beautiful books and for being such a pleasure to work with. I'd especially like to thank Gastón Castaño for his research help, encouragement and faith, and to Maia Elisa for her *joie de vivre* and love.